Love with a Few Hairs

LOVE WITH
A FEW HAIRS

Mohammed Mrabet

Taped and translated from the Moghrebi
and edited in collaboration with
Mohammed Mrabet by

Paul Bowles

CITY LIGHTS BOOKS
San Francisco

First City Lights edition, 1986
Second printing, 1992

Cover painting by Mohammed Mrabet

Library of Congress Cataloging-in-Publication Data

Mrabet, Mohammed, 1940-
    Love with a few hairs.

    Reprint. Originally published: New York:
G. Braziller, 1968.
        I. Bowles, Paul, 1910-   II. Title
        PJ7846.R3L6 1986   892'.736   86-9765
ISBN 0-87286-192-9 (pbk.)

City Lights Books are available to bookstores through our primary distributor:
Subterranean Company, P.O. Box 168, 265 S. 5th St. Monroe, OR 97456.
503-847-5274. Toll-free orders 800-274-7826. FAX 503-847-6018.
Our books are also available through library jobbers and regional distributors.
For personal orders and catalogs, please write to City Lights Books,
261 Columbus, San Francisco, CA 94133.

CITY LIGHTS BOOKS are edited by Lawrence Ferlinghetti and
Nancy J. Peters and published at the City Lights Bookstore, 261 Columbus
Avenue, San Francisco, CA 94133.

Love with a Few Hairs

There's nothing wrong with a world where you can get love with a few hairs.

1

MOHAMMED LIVED WITH Mr. David, an Englishman who owned a small hotel near the beach. His
mother had been dead for many years, but he went
often to the house where his father and brothers and
sisters lived. The only thing about Mohammed's life
which made his father sad was that during the four
years he had been living with Mr. David he had
learned to drink.

You're seventeen now, his father would say. It's
time you stopped acting like a boy. One day soon
you'll be getting married. Do you want your wife and
children to see you drunk?

Once in a while when Mohammed arrived at his
father's house he would have Mr. David with him.
Then his father's wife and his sisters would work hard
and make a big meal to serve them. At these times
Mohammed was careful not to show that he had been
drinking. Mr. David's fear was that some day the old
man might insist Mohammed stop living at the hotel
with him and return home. He did not intend to let
this happen if he could help it. Usually he brought

with him a gift or two which he would hand to Mohammed's father at the beginning of the meal. He could not understand why he never saw any of these objects again, once he had given them to him. Mohammed knew that his father generally sold them the following day, but he could not tell this to Mr. David.

You should be like the Englishman, his father would tell him. He doesn't go out into the street drunk.

Mohammed did not want any other life than the one he had with Mr. David, and so he said nothing.

During these summer months Mohammed suddenly began to come every day to visit his family. He would go up onto the roof and sit for an hour or more in the hot sun. A few doors beyond, across the street, lived a girl called Mina. Long ago, when they had been very small children, they had played together. Then he had forgotten her. This summer he had seen her grown-up for the first time. She was beautiful. Several times she had appeared in the window, but this was not enough. He wanted to talk to her. Each afternoon he sat in a chair on the roof waiting. The sun burned his skin and the flies bit him, but he went on sitting until the moment came when her face would appear in the window, and she would look out into the street as if nothing were on her mind. Then she would squint up at the roof to see if he were there. At this he would smile and bow his head once. She would laugh and vanish from the window, and he would not see her again until the next day.

When he passed Mina's house he walked more slowly, in the hope that some time she might be standing in the doorway. And one day she was there. She turned quickly to go inside, but he called to her.

2

MINA, PLEASE! I want to talk to you.

All right, she said. Talk.

He was not sure what to say. Do you remember a long time ago when we were both little, and you used to come to our house and play? You don't come any more, do you?

To your house? Are you crazy? What would your family think?

They'd be glad to see you.

She laughed. Then as if she were thinking of something else she said: Tomorrow I'm going into the city.

What time?

Around nine in the morning.

I'll be waiting for you in the garden at Sidi Boukhari, by the statue of the frog.

It was very early, but he made himself be there by the fountain the next morning when she walked up the steps. She was dressed in European clothes: a gray sweater and black slacks.

Did you sleep well? he asked her.

4

Yes, she said. I slept well.

What did you dream?

She looked down at the ground. I dreamed I was in Heaven. And you were there too.

That's a very sweet dream, he said happily. I dreamed I was sitting on a throne, and you were sitting beside me.

Allah! The King and Queen!

They walked side by side into the city. She had to buy fish and vegetables. And he bought her some bananas and apples, and two bars of chocolate. In the bus on the way back to her house he said to her: Can't I see you this afternoon? We could go to the cinema. Or a café. Or up to the mountain if you like.

She shook her head. I don't want people saying things about me.

Before they got to her house, he stopped under a tree and said to her: I want to see you later, Mina.

Yes, she said. What time?

I'll be here under this palm tree waiting for you at five this afternoon.

Ouakha, said Mina, and she walked on to her house. He stood and watched her open the door, go in, and shut it behind her. Finally he went to his father's house. He sat down and rested his elbows on the table, his head in his hands. Soon his older sister came in and looked at him.

What's wrong with you?

Nothing.

I know you! she said. There's something the matter.
I'm not sick. I'm fine.

Then why have you got your head in your hands
like that, with your eyes looking at nothing? Do you
want some lunch?

I'm not hungry. I don't want anything.

You can't do this to me! she cried. I'll be sick unless
you tell me what's wrong with you. Have you been in
a fight?

No! Not even in an argument. Nothing.

He was merely sitting, waiting for five o'clock.

A little before five he went out and found Mina
already there in the narrow street, standing under the
same palm tree.

3

THEY SAT IN the cinema, waiting to see Abd el
Wahab in *El Ouarda Beida*. Mohammed stood up.
Excuse me a minute, he said. I'll be right back. I want
to buy something.

At the tobacco shop next door he bought two bars
of chocolate. When he went back into the theater the
lights were off. He found Mina and sat down. He unwrapped one of the bars, broke off a square, and put it
into her mouth. She laughed and crunched on it.

The film began. In a little while he moved his arm
around her shoulder and rubbed his lips across her
cheek. She sat up straighter.

Mohammed, she said.

What?

Mohammed, I've never been out with a boy before.
I've never even talked to one alone before. And this is
the first time I've ever been to the cinema.

And you don't like it?

I'm afraid. People can see us.

Afraid! Do you want to drive me crazy? He hugged
her to him. I'm going to marry you, he whispered.

Mina had risen quickly and was hurrying to the back of the theater. He jumped up and ran after her, saying: What's happening? I don't understand.

Outside in the street, people were going past. Mina stopped. You're impossible, she told him. You don't know how to behave with a girl. I've always heard that, but I didn't believe it. Besides, you drink. From now on I'd rather you didn't speak to me when you go by my house. Just leave me alone.

Whatever you say, he told her. Thank you for coming with me. I'm sorry if I bothered you. I didn't know anything like this was going to happen. I'll take you home in a taxi.

I'm going by myself, she said, and walked away.

4

HE MET MR. DAVID in the entrance hall of the hotel. Come and sit down with us, said Mr. David. I want you to meet my friends.

They went into the bar. There were five Americans there, making a great deal of noise.

Yes, I'll have a whisky, said Mohammed.

He had another, and another. Mr. David was looking at him. What's the matter with you tonight, Mohammed? he said. You look sad. And why so much whisky?

I don't feel so well.

What's the matter with you?

Nothing.

Mr. David kept looking at him. Finally he leaned towards him and whispered: Do you need money?

Mohammed had not been thinking of money. Yes, he said.

Come out into the hall, Mr. David said.

There he gave Mohammed fifteen thousand francs. Mohammed thanked him and Mr. David patted him on the back. With the bills in his pocket he went out into the street, and along the seafront to the Bar Jamaica. He had another drink. As he sat looking around the bar, a friend named Mustafa came in. After they had talked a minute, Mustafa said: Mohammed, you look worried.

I don't feel much like talking. I think I'd better sit by myself.

What's the matter? Tell me about it.

I can't.

Begin, that's all.

There's a girl.

Mustafa laughed.

We were in the cinema, and when I put my arm around her she began telling me how she'd never talked to a man before. She'd never even been to see a film before. She told me I was no good. Then she went home.

Mustafa laughed again. Is that all?

For me it's something. I'm not twenty-seven like you. I've got to get her back.

I know a woman, Mustafa said. A witch who lives in Beni Makada.

You think she could do something?

I know she can. I've used her. We can go out there now.

They paid the barman and walked down into the Avenida de España. It was nearly evening. A cab came past, and they stopped it and climbed in.

5

THEY DROVE ALL the way through Beni Makada, to the other end of the town where the radio towers stood. There were rows of small shacks stretching across the fields. Mustafa stopped the taxi and Mohammed paid the driver. Then Mustafa knocked on a door made of oil tins pressed flat. An old woman wrapped in rags opened it and stepped out.

What is it?

Can we talk to you? asked Mustafa.

She looked at him closely and let them in. Sit down, she said, pointing to an old mattress in the corner. There was a torn reed mat on the floor, and a blanket that had been folded and pushed between the mattress and the wall. Everything was gray with dirt. The smell in the room made Mohammed feel sick.

The woman sat on the floor. What do you want, son? she said, looking at Mohammed.

Lalla, I'm in love with a girl. I want to marry her. I don't want to do her any harm.

I see, she said.

The trouble is, she doesn't love me.

I can do it, she told him. But it's a little expensive.

How much would it be, Lalla? More or less?

It would cost ten thousand francs.

I'll pay you ten thousand, Lalla.

One thing, she said, pointing her finger at him.

What's that?

You'll have to bring me a piece of something she's worn, or a few of her hairs. One or the other.

How am I going to get her hair? Or her clothes, either? It's impossible.

There must be somebody who goes into her house now and then. You can manage it, she told him.

Then he thought of a twelve-year-old boy who was a cousin of Mina's. The boy was always going in and out of the house.

Yes, Lalla, he said. I'll bring you something. If I don't come tomorrow I'll be here the day after.

Yes. She got up and opened the door. Good-bye.

They went down the road.

I'm going to talk to little Larbi, said Mohammed. He'll do anything for money. I'll see you in the morning at the café.

6

AT THE CROSSROADS they said good-bye, and Mohammed started walking up the hill towards Mstakhoche, where his father lived. On the way he saw a small boy standing in the street. He sent him to the house of Larbi's parents, telling him to bring Larbi right away. Then he stood in the street waiting. When Larbi arrived he asked him if it were not true that he went nearly every day to Mina's house.

Yes, said Larbi. Almost every day.

Here it is, said Mohammed. You're going to do something for me, and I'm going to pay you.

What do I have to do?

You have to cut off a little piece of one of Mina's dresses or something. Or you look in her comb and see if there are any hairs in it. If there are, I want them.

Good, said the boy. I'll bring it.

Larbi went off. In Mina's house he waited until he saw her combing her hair. When she went into the other room he seized the comb and pulled out several long silky hairs. Then he folded them in his hand and carried them back to Mohammed, who was waiting at his father's house.

Mohammed took out five hundred francs. Here, he told him.

The next morning he went down to the café.

Good morning, said Mustafa. Did you get it?

Larbi brought me some hairs. I paid him enough so he'll be quiet. Here they are. Let's go and see the witch.

They found a taxi and went to Beni Makada. The old woman let them in. They sat down on the mattress and Mohammed gave her the hairs. She pulled out a cloth sack and began to search through it for things: packets of herbs and envelopes full of fingernails and teeth and bits of dried skin. She shook things out onto a sheet of paper, along with Mina's hairs. Then over it all she poured a powder that looked like dirt. She folded everything inside the paper and put it into a tin. A long string of words kept coming out of her mouth. She threw benzoin onto the hot coals of the brazier and she put the tin in the center of the fire, stirring it for a long time until it all had become a black powder. When it had cooled off she poured it into a paper and folded the paper into a packet.

She handed the packet to Mohammed. Take this. Pour the powder outside the door of her house. When you've left it there, don't look down at it. Walk away.

But when? said Mohammed. At night or in the daytime?

You can do it whenever you like.

He put the folded paper into his pocket and handed her five thousand francs.

Here's five thousand, he said. As soon as it's worked, I'll bring you the other five.

I see, she said.

And if it doesn't work I'm coming back here to get my five thousand.

The old woman laughed.

7

BY TWO O'CLOCK in the morning Mohammed was drunk. He had stayed in the Bar Jamaica the whole evening. Now he left it, and walked along the avenues on his way out to Mstakhoche. When he got to his street there was no one in sight. At Mina's door he pulled the paper out of his pocket. The street light did not shine on the front of the house. He knelt down and sprinkled the powder on the ground by the door. Then he stood up and walked on to his father's house.

In the morning when Mina got up she did her work, washing dishes and glasses and scrubbing the floor. Finally she started to make her mother's lunch. She opened the door and went out with a pail to get water from the fountain. And she had to step over the powder.

When he saw her standing in the doorway for a minute, Mohammed went out and walked slowly past her house. Good morning, he said. But she pretended not to have heard, and he walked on.

At the end of the day, when he had changed his

clothes, he went back to Mstakhoche and strolled in the street, back and forth in front of her house. Soon he caught sight of her in the window. When she saw that he had noticed her she began to laugh.

He stood still near the window. What are you laughing at? he asked her.

You!

Why? What's funny about me?

Nothing. But this morning you said hello to me and I didn't answer. And I was afraid you'd gone away angry.

Angry? I went away feeling fine. I said good morning and you didn't. I was thinking all afternoon of how happy I was.

I'm glad you were happy all afternoon, at least, she said.

And now, if I say good evening, can you say it back to me?

Yes, I can, now, she told him.

Mohammed decided then that the spell was beginning to work. Can you come out for a walk? he asked her.

There's nobody in the house. I have to stay here until my mother and father come back.

How about next Friday at five? Can you come out?

Pass by the park at Sidi Boukhari, she said. I might be sitting on a bench there.

Good.

There were some flower pots in the window. Mina

disappeared inside. A moment later she was in the window again with a pair of scissors in her hand. She cut a white carnation from one of the plants, kissed it, and tossed it to him.

He caught it, and raised it to his lips. Good-bye.

Good-bye, she said.

Sitting in a café, Mohammed held the flower in his hand, thinking of how far away Friday afternoon was.

8

ON FRIDAY AFTERNOON Mohammed went and knocked on the door of Mr. David's office. Mr. David was typing at his desk.

What are you writing?

A letter to my father in England. Did you want something?

I need some money, Mohammed said. He knew that Mr. David liked him to ask outright rather than give him hints.

How much?

Fifteen thousand.

Fine. He took out the bills and gave them to him.

And I wonder if you could do me a favor? Mohammed went on.

What's that?

I wonder if I could take the car?

I suppose so. But don't get drunk.

Of course not, said Mohammed.

When he drew up at the park Mina saw him coming. She got up and walked towards him. They drove off by way of the mountain. It was midsummer and the air smelled sweet when they went through the pine forests.

We had fun when we were little, didn't we? said Mohammed. Remember how we used to play in the mud? And go to the park and hide behind the trees, and run out and splash in the fountain there? We'd pull up the plants and chase each other and have fights with them. Do you remember?

Yes, she said. And the time you hit me in the head with a stone?

You haven't forgotten that?

They began to laugh.

He parked in front of the café there at the top of the cliff at El Achaqal, and they went inside and sat down. He ordered a Coca-Cola for Mina and a beer for himself.

Presently she said: Mohammed, why do you drink?

I have to, he said. I live with a Nazarene in a place that's always full of Nazarenes, Americans, Englishmen, Frenchmen. They come in and order drinks at the bar, and then they ask me if I want a drink. I can't tell them I'd rather have a coffee or a tea or a Coca-Cola. If an American offers me a whisky I can't take anything but a whisky. Isn't that right?

Yes. That's true.

But some day, he went on, I'm going to stop. I can live without drinking. That's what I really want.

You're right, she told him.

Mina, if I wanted to marry you, would you marry me?

She was laughing. Mohammed, I like you a lot, she said. But I'm afraid.

Of what?

Of you.

Of me? But why? We wouldn't do anything together until we'd been to the notaries and the qadi and had the papers all made out.

I think we ought to go, said Mina.

He got up and paid. They drove back to the city along the airport road.

Mohammed, she was saying. I don't feel like going back to my house. I don't want the day to end.

I don't want it to end either, he said. But you've got to go home now, or your family will be wondering what's happened. Can I see you next week? I could meet you early, and we could go wherever you like.

Perhaps we could eat at El Achaqal, she said. I love to eat on the beach, the way the Nazarenes do.

All right.

I'll meet you at two o'clock in the park, she told him.

9

EARLY THE NEXT Sunday morning while it was still cool Mohammed was buying bread from the bread-sellers in the street. Then he went to the market and bought tuna fish, olives, hard-boiled eggs and bananas. He put everything into the car and drove home to put on his bathing suit, and get a towel and some sun lotion.

She was waiting on the same bench. This time he drove all the way down to the shore at El Achaqal, and they sat on the sand near the big rocks. It was a fine day. The beach was covered with English and American tourists. The sun was very hot and the sea was as flat and smooth as a highway. He spread a big towel at the foot of the rocks while Mina took off her slacks and her skirt. Underneath she was wearing a bikini. He undressed and took out the jar of sun cream.

Mina stretched out face down on the towel, and he began to rub the cream over her back and legs. Then she turned over so he could spread it on the rest of her. When he got to her ribs she laughed and sat up.

They lay side by side on the towel in the sun.

Mohammed, she said.

What, Mina?

What would it be like if one of us should die, I wonder?

Die! He rolled his head towards her. If you died I'd be lost. And if I should die I suppose you'd be sad, too. Let's not die. Let's stay alive.

He sat up and lit a cigarette. She looked at him.

Mohammed, she said.

What?

That cigarette you're smoking. What does it do to you?

Oh, nothing. It's only a vice. It doesn't give any pleasure. And it's bad for the body. But a man has to have a vice, or he might as well be dead. Some drink, some smoke kif or tobacco. Some have to be with a different woman every day. Each one has something.

But you've got two, she said. You're got tobacco and alcohol too.

No, that's not true, he told her. I only drink when I'm nervous. Cigarettes are different.

Let me try, she said, sitting up and reaching for the cigarette.

You won't like it.

She took it and puffed on it once. Then she began to choke and cough.

You're right, she said.

They got up and started to chase each other along

the beach. He let her run far ahead of him so he could watch her. Finally he caught her. For a while they played ball with a group of Spaniards. Then they ran on, into the ocean. They waded out until the water was up to their shoulders, and Mohammed tried to pull her further, but she did not know how to swim. He did his best to show her how, supporting her from beneath on the palms of his hands. The sun glistened like fire on the water all around them. Soon she was tired.

Back by the rocks, they dried themselves.

Wait, he said. I'm going up to the café a minute. He climbed up the side of the cliff and in a few minutes was down again with two bottles of beer and a Coca-Cola. Then they brought out the food.

As they were eating, she suddenly exclaimed: What a vice! Do you have to drink beer every time you sit down to eat?

If I don't I can't eat.

I know, she said, shaking her head. Some people have to have wine with their meals. But most people just drink water.

They finished eating and stretched out on the sand in the sun.

Why don't we get dressed and go up to the café? he said.

In a little while.

If your mother knew you were here with me at El Achaqal, would she make trouble?

You know she would.

He touched her face with his fingers. Then he put his arm around her and pulled her to him, to kiss the spots he had touched with his fingers. When her arms went around him, he kissed her lips. Suddenly she was saying: Mohammed, I love you. I want to be with you always. Every minute.

The spell is working, thought Mohammed.

They climbed the path that went back and forth between the rocks, up the side of the cliff. He went first, holding her arm to keep her from falling. In the café they drank black coffee.

I'm going to take you home now, he said. I've got something to do in town.

She sighed.

As they drove past the cows and camels in the fields beside the road, it occurred to him that he would like to know more about how the spell had worked. You've got to tell me something, he said.

What's that?

Tell me. When did you first know you liked me? A while ago you wouldn't even speak to me. Isn't that true?

Yes, Mohammed. But there are thousands like us. They argue and quarrel, and in the end they fall in love. If two people haven't fought they don't know each other. It's better to fight at the beginning than later. It's true I didn't like you at the cinema. And whatever I said then, I'm sorry I said it.

That's all finished. You didn't say anything so bad.

You were angry, so you went out of the theater. I couldn't force you to stay there. Besides, I thought you might change your mind some day.

He stopped the car in a side street not far from Mina's house. People walking by stared at them. He kissed her cheek, and then her hand, and she got out.

Next Sunday, can I meet you? he said.

I have to go somewhere with my family.

And the week after?

Yes.

At half past four, or five?

Half past four.

10

MOHAMMED WAS STANDING in a bar on the beach in the city having a beer. Mustafa came in.

So here you are! You've forgotten all about us. What news of the girl friend?

Beautiful, said Mohammed. He laughed.

Have you been back to pay the witch?

No, but I will.

And the powder really worked?

Worked! I just this minute left her. What are you having?

Beer, said Mustafa. Soon he looked at Mohammed and said: You're not really going to marry her, are you?

Is that what you think? Don't you know what love is? When I was this big I used to take care of her. I've always loved her.

Mohammed went on drinking. After a while he was saying, again and again: She could die or I could die. But there's nobody alive who could pull us apart.

That's the way to talk! said Mustafa. Marry her, get yourself a good house, and fill it with young ones.

This is a hard world. You might as well try to be happy.

Mustafa did not really believe this, but they were drinking in a bar.

Incha'Allah, said Mohammed, already feeling happy. He was thinking: There's nothing wrong with a world where you can get love with a few hairs. It's wonderful!

11

LATE ONE AFTERNOON Mohammed and Mr. David were sitting in the garden having a drink together. Mohammed was nervous. He was putting off asking if he might take the big car. Mr. David had a Mercedes as well as the Volkswagen which Mohammed usually borrowed. When the moment came to say the words, he found himself asking for the Volkswagen. Of course, said Mr. David. But remember we're going to a party tonight. And don't forget what we were talking about. Be careful of that girl.

Mohammed hurried out and got into the car. He drove to Sidi Boukhari and picked up Mina. It was a hot mid-summer evening, and he felt like being in the country under the sky and smelling the plants. He drove on, out to Boubana, and stopped by the river. They got out and sat down, leaning against the trunk of a high eucalyptus. There was a soft light in the sky, and the air under the trees here by the river was cool.

He passed his hands over her hair. It's like silk, he said. He kissed her lips. The kisses ran between them like the waves of the sea.

He drew back and looked at her. Mina, some day I'm going to eat you.

She stared into his eyes. Eat me now, she said. Do whatever you want. Anything. Everything. Whatever you say is all right. Kill me and cut me into pieces if you feel like it.

Mohammed sat straighter. This was surely the spell working, he thought. And he remembered that he had not gone back and paid the witch the other five thousand francs. The words Mina was saying could be the old woman's way of making trouble for him. He resolved to go and pay her in the morning.

Get up, he said to Mina. Let's go.

What for? It's still early.

It's half past six. We should go. Your mother's going to start asking you where you've been.

You're right, she said, and got up slowly.

They walked back to the car, and he drove her home.

That night he lay awake thinking. There was something disturbing about Mina's words. For two weeks he kept away from Mstakhoche. In the meantime he told Mr. David about the witch, and was astonished to see how delighted Mr. David was to hear that he had worked magic on the girl. He wanted to know all about it. At the end he gave him the five thousand francs, and told him to be sure and go to pay the old woman.

At the witch's shack, before giving her the money,

he told her about Mina's behavior, and asked her if she could not reduce the effect of the spell a bit.

The old woman laughed. You asked me to make her fall in love with you, and I did it. Now manage it the way you like. Either you want her or you don't.

He paid her and went away dissatisfied. At least, he thought, the witch would not be working against him now.

12

FINALLY MOHAMMED WENT back to Mina's house at Mstakhoche and arranged to see her the following Sunday evening. When he met her in the park she was wearing a bright green satin evening dress, black shoes with very high heels, and two heavy gold bracelets. Her hair fell down lightly around her shoulders. When he had looked a while at her, he said: Come with me to the hotel. I want you to meet my friend. I think you'll like him.

They got into the car and drove to the center of the city. He parked on the Boulevard and took Mina into a shop. The Indian came up to him.

What can I do?

I want to see some ladies' wristwatches, he told him.

Yes. We have them. And he began to pour watches on top of the counter.

Mohammed looked and said: Not this sort. I want something good.

Yes. We have them too. He brought out some watches from behind a screen. These are gold.

Mohammed picked up a thin square watch. This is a beauty, he told Mina. How much is this one?

That is seventeen thousand, said the Indian.

That's the one we want. He tried to pay fifteen thousand, but the Indian would not listen. Then he paid him sixteen thousand, and they went out to the car. When they were sitting inside, he handed Mina the parcel.

You shouldn't waste your money this way, Mohammed. I love you anyway, without presents.

No, he said, We have to go to good places, and you have to wear good things. I don't want to see you in old clothes with no shape to them, or look at your legs and see a pair of old worn-out shoes. I want you to look better than anybody else.

Thank you. You're very sweet. She kissed him, and people walking past stared into the car. He started the motor and they drove off.

When they got to the hotel, Mr. David stood in the doorway looking into the street.

I want to introduce my fiancée, Mohammed told him. Mina, this is Mr. David.

Enchanté, mademoiselle, said Mr. David, looking up and down the street. *Je suis content que vous soyez venue. Entrez, entrez.*

Mina did not understand anything but Arabic. Mohammed pushed her ahead of him, and Mr. David led them into the bar without looking at them. The room was very smoky and full of Americans. Mohammed

33

presented Mina to the Americans who were friends of his. There was a good deal of laughter among the Nazarenes, but Mr. David did not laugh. Then the two sat down at one of the tables. The Americans tried to talk to Mina in Spanish. She smiled.

What are you going to have? Mohammed asked her.

A limonada, she said.

Limonada!

Yes.

You can't get that here. All you can get is things like whisky or cognac. But I'll bring you something that won't leave any smell on your breath. It's sweet.

All right.

Mohammed got up and went over to the bar. He filled a glass with Cinzano and put in a maraschino cherry. Then he took it over to her. Try this, he said.

He got himself a whisky and brought it back to the table. She was drinking her Cinzano and liking it. When she had finished it he got her another, and then another, until she had drunk five. By this time she was talking very fast.

Mr. David came over to the table and bent down to speak into Mohammed's ear. You've got to take that girl home, he told him. She's very drunk.

No, no, Mohammed said. She's not drunk yet. She's just playing.

Mina jumped up and ran in front of Mr. David, out into the middle of the floor. She began to sing and

34

dance. Between dances she went on talking in Arabic.

Mohammed watched Mr. David and his American friends. When he saw that they were all tired of Mina, he got up. Let's go, he said, taking hold of her arm. I'm going to take you home.

13

MOHAMMED HAD MINA say good night to each one of the Americans, and then he led her outside. When they were in the car, she turned to him and said: Mohammed, there's only one person in the world I love.

Me too, he said.

But you don't know who it is, she went on.

Who is it?

You don't know? The one person in the world I love? You don't know who it is?

No.

It's you, Mohammed. She laid her head on his shoulder. You're the first boy I've ever loved.

Mohammed started the motor. And I could never love any other girl the way I love you, he told her. Nobody. Nobody else can make me feel the way you do, Mina. And now we're going to the pharmacy and I'm going to get you some medicine to clear your head. And then we'll stop at a café and have some black coffee with lemon in it, and by the time you get home you'll feel all right.

Mina did not seem to understand what he was saying. She only shook her head back and forth. I'm going to stay with you, she told him. Always. I'm not going home. What am I going to do at home? I want to be with you.

With a pill and some coffee you'll feel better, Mina. You've got to go home. If you stay with me now, what's going to happen? Nothing but trouble. And by the time it's over we won't even love each other any longer.

But she went on shaking her head. It's no use, Mohammed, she told him. From the way she said it, he felt that she was right, that no one could stop her from doing what she had decided to do.

Ouakha, he said, and started the car up the hill with a great noise. He drove beyond Mstakhoche to the very edge of the town, where he had a small room that he kept for nights when he felt like staying up and having a good time with his friends. He unlocked the door.

It was damp inside.

They went in and sat down, he on the chair and she on the bed. There was a bottle of whisky on the table. He poured himself a drink.

Give me some, she said. I want to drink whisky. I've never drunk whisky.

Whisky's no good for you, he told her. If you begin to drink whisky you're going to throw up. You'll feel terrible.

But she insisted. I want to try it, she kept saying.

Mohammed stood up. I'm going out and get you that medicine, and you're going to take it. And then you're going home.

Mina lay back on the bed. I'm going to sleep here. And I'm going to drink whisky.

All right, he said angrily. And he took a glass, poured whisky in and added some water, and handed it to her.

She got up off the bed with the glass in her hand and started to walk across the room. When she had nearly reached the chair where he sat, she began to sway. He jumped up and caught her.

You get into bed and rest, he told her, stroking her hair. I'm going to sleep in the chair.

No, you're not, she said. You're going to sleep in the bed with me.

No, no, no! He was looking away from her, across the room.

Both of us. She held his waist more tightly.

Good! he said so suddenly and so loud that she let go of him and tried to look at his face. He walked to the other side of the room and stood there with his hands in his pockets.

Mina leaned on the chair and began to undress. She took off her green evening gown and her *soutien-gorge*, and stood there in her underpants. Then she got into the bed. He went back and sat in the chair, and slowly drank the whisky, until there was none left. He was wishing that she had not drunk so much. He wanted to feel that it was he who had decided everything, and instead he felt that Mina was doing exactly as she pleased with him. How can she want to sleep here in this dirty bed? he thought.

He got up and took off his jacket, then his shirt, then his trousers. He hesitated, then got into the bed, still wearing his shorts. As soon as he lay down she put her arm over him. He seized her and kissed her. They said I love you, back and forth. Then he said: It was a bad thing you did, coming here.

Don't talk about it, she said.

Soon he ran his hand down her thigh and slipped off her underwear. Then with more kisses he finally went in, and from being a girl Mina became a woman. She hugged him very tight. And that way they stayed until it was morning.

14

WHEN MINA GOT out of bed she looked down and saw the streaks of blood on the sheet. She sat down again on the edge of the bed and burst into tears. Mohammed opened his eyes.

It's a sin, what you've done, she finally said between sobs. You made me get drunk. If you hadn't given me those drinks I never would have come here. What am I going to do now? I can't go home.

She went on weeping. Mohammed sat up and put his arm around her. Don't cry. We'll get married, he said.

She wiped her eyes. I'm afraid. Sooner or later you'll leave me. It's just a game for you, but everybody's going to be against me. My father'll kill me. I know he'll do something terrible. And if the police hear about it, they'll make trouble for you.

Mina, he said. I swear by the food we've eaten together and the blood on this sheet, you've got nothing to worry about. You're going to live with me. Now lie down and stop thinking about it. I'll be right back. Stay here in bed.

He went out, and shortly he came back with fruit and vegetables and meat. And he had bought a live chicken. Mina was still in bed. He took the chicken out into the street and cut its throat. Then he came in and began to make chicken broth for Mina. It took a long time. When the meal was ready, he carried the table across the room, and they ate sitting side by side on the edge of the bed. As soon as they had finished, Mohammed said: Why don't we go out?

I couldn't. I'm too tired.

I'll bring the car.

Leave me here, she told him. I'm going to sleep a while. You go wherever you want. She lay down on the bed.

I'll be back, he said.

He walked down to the Boulevard and went into a shop. He bought two nightgowns and three bathrobes and two pairs of bedroom slippers lined with white fur and a large bottle of Eau de Cologne and a box of bath powder and several bars of bath soap. When he got back to the mahal he found her having coffee.

Wouldn't you like some? she asked him.

Good.

She poured it out for him. What's in all those packages? she said.

I brought you some things. I don't know whether you'll like them.

She put one of the packages on the table, opened it, and pulled out the nightgowns.

Mohammed, she said laughing. I'm so happy! Thank you. Nobody else could make me so happy.

It's nothing. Just a few clothes. He took her hand. Later we'll live better than this, and I'll get you better things than these. We have plenty of time ahead of us.

Mina was looking at him and shaking her head. I didn't know you were going to be so nice to me. I thought you didn't care. But now I know you do love me. We really will get married, won't we?

Of course.

But Mohammed, she said, her voice sounding frightened again.

What?

My father and mother must be looking for me. Suppose they find out I'm with you?

Her words made Mohammed feel very uncomfortable, but he said: Leave that to me. Don't think about it.

That evening when it had got dark he managed to make Mina agree that if he could get the car she would take a ride with him.

Mr. David said nothing, but it seemed to Mohammed that his glance was not very friendly.

Yes. Of course, he said after a moment. Take it.

Mohammed parked the car in the street at Mstakhoche and walked to the mahal. Mina put on her green evening gown, and they walked together through the alleys until they got to the car. As he was helping Mina to get in, he saw an old woman in a gray djellaba stop and look closely at them. He shut the car door. Then he went round to the other side and got in. The old woman was still standing there, staring at Mina.

Trouble, he thought. But he said nothing, and they took their ride.

15

THE OLD WOMAN went directly to Mina's house. I've just seen your daughter! She was getting into a car in the Souq el Bqar with Mohammed, that boy who lives here across the street, and they drove away together.

What!

A few minutes ago.

Her father's spent all night and all day looking for her. It's a terrible tragedy. These girls today are the worst ever. God help all women with daughters! Bitches and dogs in the street, that's what the young people are today.

When Mina's father came in, Husband, she said to him, Mina's with that Mohammed from across the street.

What are you saying?

Hadija was just here. She saw her getting into his car.

He's taken her to that filthy Christian hotel down there, said Si Ahmed, and he started out at once for the hotel, walking as fast as he could. About forty-five minutes later he arrived, and asked the night watchman for Mohammed.

Mohammed had just left Mina in the mahal at Mstakhoche after their ride, and gone back to the hotel with the car. In a moment he came out of the bar. His heart sank when he saw who had asked to see him.

Salaamou aleikoum.

Aleikoum salaam.

Is your name Mohammed Ouriagli?

Yes, he said, keeping his eyes narrow. He felt that they had opened too wide.

My daughter is with you?

Yes.

And how do you explain that? shouted Si Ahmed, waving his cane.

We're in love with each other. We want to get married.

Garbage. That's what you are, said Mina's father. Where is she?

She's not here, said Mohammed. Tomorrow at twelve o'clock I'll come to your house and take you to see her.

You'll do much more than that, said Si Ahmed. Then he went out, talking to himself.

Mr. David tried to keep Mohammed from going out that night. I know what you're doing, he told him, and you're going to ruin your health. Why don't we take a bottle of champagne into the bedroom and play some music?

Mohammed did not answer. His face grew red and he looked at the floor, and Mr. David knew that there was no way of keeping him in.

It was late when Mohammed arrived at the mahal in Mstakhoche. He opened the door. Mina was sitting in the chair in the center of the room, waiting for him. He shut the door behind him, and she jumped up and threw herself into his arms.

There was a strong warm wind that night. Mohammed opened the window and stood leaning out for a moment. Then he got into his pyjamas. Mina was already in bed.

Lying beside her, he stared at her for a long time, thinking of many things. As he looked at her, her face seemed to change shape and take on many different expressions. The one face became many faces. She had large eyes with long lashes, and her eyebrows were high and arched. He glanced down at her body. It was small and plump. He slid his arms around her and began to kiss her eyes, her nose and her cheeks.

Mina. Mina. Without you there'd be nothing, he was saying. You're got to stay with me always. If God would only help us we could get out of this country and go somewhere else. Some place far away, like America or France or London. No people always making trouble. He could not bring himself to tell her that he had seen her father and was going to bring him to the mahal in the morning.

You know, even after we're married, your family's never going to like me, because of what we've done, he said.

Don't talk about it! She began to cover his lips with kisses, so that he could not go on speaking. The warm wind blew in over them, and made a noise in the canes across the alley. Later they fell asleep.

In the morning when Mohammed was dressed and ready to go out, he turned to her and said: What would you do if your father should come here?

Here! He can't!

I just wondered, said Mohammed.

He'd beat me! He'd kill me!

Don't worry. I won't let that happen, he told her. I'll be back around noon.

16

MOHAMMED WALKED IN the morning sun to his father's house. He had not been there this early in the morning for a long time. His father's wife opened the door. He went inside and found his father sitting with his brothers.

Father, he said.

Yes.

A girl called Mina, the one who lives across the street. You know who I mean?

His father's wife looked at him. Yes, she said.

We've got to get married. Can I have my wedding party here in the house? That's what I wanted to say, to see whether you were willing or not.

His father's wife said nothing. She went on looking at him.

Mohammed! cried his father. Do you know what you're doing?

What am I doing?

His father sat back and was silent for a moment. Then he said: I have only one thing to say to you. If you marry that girl, don't bother to come back to this house again. And don't take the trouble to speak to me if you see me in the street, either, because I won't be your father. Think about it.

Mohammed went out of the house and sat on the grass above the reservoir for an hour or so. It occurred to him that he had often heard his father speak with scorn of Mina's mother as a whore. He may be right, Mohammed thought. He may have good reasons for keeping the families apart. Then he remembered something that Mr. David had told him many times: The day you get married you can say good-bye to me. He had never paid the threat any attention because he had never thought of getting married. Now, however, he was convinced that Mr. David meant what he said. He could not understand Mr. David. Sometimes he complained about Mohammed's girls, and sometimes he did not seem to care. But he always urged him to get rid of whatever girl he had at the moment, and look for a new one.

He got up and walked to Mina's house. Si Ahmed was waiting for him, and Mina's mother was in her veil and haik. The three of them set out on foot for the mahal. They did not speak on the way.

When Mohammed unlocked the door, Mina was standing just inside. Her mother rushed into the room and took her in her arms, and they both burst into tears.

Oh, my baby! My precious! Why did you run away? Why have you made us wait so long?

They both went on crying. Then Mina saw her father, and she ran to him and kissed him. Forgive me! she cried. Forgive me! I know it's a terrible thing. But I love Mohammed and I've got to stay with him. We're going to get married.

As she spoke, Si Ahmed was looking around at the furniture in the mahal. He patted her shoulder. Thank God no one knows about it, he said. It'll come out all right. We'll arrange everything.

Sit down, said Mohammed. He was growing more nervous each moment. Mina, get some coffee for your father. He took out a pack of Olympics and offered one to Si Ahmed.

Si Ahmed lighted the cigarette, sat back, and said: What are we going to do now?

Mohammed took a deep breath. I can't marry her, he said.

Mina's father stood up. You'll marry her or I'll have you in court! he shouted.

You can put me in front of the firing squad if you like, Mohammed cried. I can't marry her.

Without looking at Mina he ran out into the street.

17

THAT AFTERNOON MR. David was at a cocktail party. There was no one in the hotel but Mohammed and Ali the dishwasher. About four o'clock a jeep drew up in front of the door. Mina's father came into the bar, and there were three policemen with him.

Good afternoon, said the policemen. Then they said to Mohammed: Come with us.

Yes, said Mohammed. He went out with them and got into the jeep. They drove him to the Mendoubia and left him in an office there.

Sit down, the official said.

You've got to marry this girl, he told Mohammed.

Mohammed talked a long while. At the end he said he could not marry Mina because his father would not permit it.

The official wrote down the information about him and his family. He took up the telephone. While he was still talking, a man came in and led Mohammed into another room. He sat here alone for fifteen minutes or so. Then two policemen opened the door and beckoned to him. As he went through the doorway, they said: Put your hands out.

Why? Why are you putting handcuffs on me?

They pushed him into a van with some other prisoners and took him to the jail in the Casbah. There they left him alone in a small room with no light in it.

The sixth day after lunch, a guard came and opened the door. Come out, he told him. Mohammed went out into the corridor.

We can't have you sitting there in the dark all the time, said the guard. We thought you ought to get out into the sun for a while. Come up on the roof.

There was no other prisoner in sight on the roof. Wherever Mohammed walked, the guard walked with him.

You must have a good job, the guard said.

Yes, said Mohammed.

I've seen this girl, you know, said the guard. She's a real beauty! Why don't you want to marry her? I don't understand you. It's the only way of getting out of here, anyway. You'll be here for two months before your trial. And then they can give you two years. At least marriage doesn't take that long.

Mohammed listened to the guard's words, and felt his heart sink. He had thought the entire thing would take a month at the most.

I'm telling you the truth, the guard told him. I have your papers downstairs. It says on them two months until the trial, and after that they send you to Casablanca or Larache. They won't leave you here. The only way you can save yourself is to marry her. That way you get out of here, stay with her a month or two and beat her up every night. She'll be glad to escape. I feel sorry for you, young and strong like this, wasting your life breaking rocks in jail. You'll be in and out of the hospital for the rest of your life. That's what happens if you stay in places like this.

I know, said Mohammed.

He passed most of the night thinking about it.

Every day someone came for him and took him up onto the roof to let him walk around in the sun, but he did not catch sight of the guard who had talked to him.

One day Mr. David arrived at the jail, asking to see Mohammed. What is this? he demanded.

I can't tell you, said Mohammed.

Tell me, for God's sake! I can help you. I can get you lawyers.

You can't help me. It's no use. It's the girl I brought to see you that night at the hotel.

I knew it! cried Mr. David. I knew she'd get you in trouble! Whatever it is, you can't just stay in jail. I won't let you stay on in this place. You've only been here two weeks, and already you look terrible! Your health will be ruined.

The visit is over, said the guard.

Don't get me any lawyers or anything, Mohammed called after Mr. David.

Time passed. He had been in jail a month. One day when they took him up onto the roof, he met the guard who had taken him up the first day. He was standing by the railing, looking down into the courtyard. Then he saw Mohammed.

Good morning, 125. How are you?

Mohammed greeted him. As the guard was about to go downstairs, Mohammed said: Can I speak with you?

Of course. What is it?

I'm sick of this place. Alone in a dark room. Always alone. I can't stand any more of it. I'll explode. I want to marry the girl.

The guard laughed. Tonight you'll sleep at home. I promise you.

Mohammed went downstairs to the office with him while he telephoned to the Mendoubia. Then he went back to his room. Later in the day the guard came and opened the door. Let's go, he said.

They went out and got into a station wagon, and the guard went with him to the Mendoubia. In the office of the oukil ed doula the official asked him: And why did you refuse the other time? You wouldn't have had to spend a whole month sitting up there. Look at you now, sad and dirty.

Mohammed was angry, and he looked at the floor. I wanted to see what jail was like, he said.

Now you know, said the official. The secretary handed Mohammed a pen. Sign here, he told him.

You're free now. Be here in this office tomorrow morning at nine o'clock.

18

MOHAMMED WENT OUT into the street with his filthy clothes and his long hair. He took a taxi at the Zoco de Fuera and went straight to the hotel. Mr. David was sitting with some friends. When he saw Mohammed he sprang up and took him in his arms. Then he began to cry.

Give me some money, said Mohammed. I've got to pay the taxi driver.

Mr. David excused himself from his friends and took Mohammed out to his bedroom in the garden.

Tell me everything, Mohammed. How did you get out?

If I tell you, you're going to be very upset, said Mohammed.

Why? What is it?

I've got to get married. Then he told him the whole story. At the end, he said: But it won't take long. The way I'm going to treat her, she'll be begging to leave.

Mr. David's face brightened a little. There's nothing else to do, he said.

You're going to be very sad, Mohammed told him.

No, I'm not. I'm just happy to see you now. He hugged Mohammed and kissed him. Mohammed was very good to him, and kissed him and made him feel happier. Then he said: Please. I want to take a bath. I've got to shave and go out and get a haircut, too.

He had been alone for so long that he felt like seeing his family. From the barber's he went to Mstakhoche. If his father asked him where he had been, he was going to tell him he had been on a trip with Mr. David. He did not intend to mention Mina.

There was no one at home but two of his brothers. He sat and talked with them for a while, and then he went up the street to Mina's house.

Mina herself opened the door. As soon as she had kissed him, she began to weep. Her mother came in, looked at Mohammed angrily, and sat down in the corner. When her father appeared, he said: How was the jail?

Terrible, said Mohammed. I decided I'd rather marry Mina.

Good, said Si Ahmed.

Tomorrow you're supposed to go down to the Mendoubia, Mohammed told him. At nine o'clock in the morning. That's all I came to tell you. I've got to go now.

I'm going with you, said Mina, jumping up.

No, you're not. You stay here with your mother.

Mohammed went back to the hotel. That night he slept with Mr. David. Early in the morning he was in the market buying food. At nine o'clock he went to the Mendoubia and met Mina and her parents outside the big gate. The secretary spoke with each one of them, and when they left, he gave them three papers, one for Mohammed, one for Mina and one for her father. Then they all went to the mahal in Msta-khoche. Mohammed had invited them for lunch.

Mina and her mother made tea for Si Ahmed and Mohammed, and then they went into the kitchen to prepare lunch.

How much do you earn where you work? Si Ahmed asked Mohammed.

Mohammed hesitated. I don't know, he said. It depends on the tips. Some days are good. Some days are bad.

The Nazarenes must pay you quite a lot. You live well.

Come and sit down, said Mina, and we'll eat. They got up and went to sit at the taifor. Mina poured water over their hands, and then they began to eat.

When this accident happened with Mina, said her mother, why didn't you let us know? You could have sent somebody to tell us she was alive, at least.

Satan didn't want it that way, said Mohammed. But the wedding will make it exactly as if nothing had happened. As long as nobody talks about it. Mina must have a big party. Tomorrow we'll go and arrange the papers. My father mustn't know anything or he'll make trouble. And Mina must stay with you until after the party.

You're right, said Si Ahmed. Everybody must be

very calm and do everything the way it ought to be done.

When they finished eating, Mina carried in the pitcher and the bowl, and poured water over their hands. Then she brought the tea tray and made tea for them.

Mina, said her mother. We've got to go now, and you've got to come with us.

But I haven't seen Mohammed in a month! Mina cried.

And what do you think people are going to say if you stay here?

Si Ahmed got up. You come with us, he said, and all three of them went out.

19

MOHAMMED WAS SITTING in the Café Central that
afternoon, thinking. A deaf and dumb man was going
from table to table, waving his arms, asking for
money. Monhammed gave him a coin and smiled. He
was happy that Mr. David had not complained that he
was getting married, but he had not yet mentioned the
money. It was going to cost a great deal. Mohammed
planned to remind Mr. David of the money he had
been willing to spend for lawyers to get him out of
jail.

Soon he caught sight of Mustafa going through the
square.

Mustafa! Mustafa! he cried. Come here. I want to
talk to you.

Mustafa stopped and sat down at the table.

I need a house. Do you know of one?

A house! What do you want of a house?

Mohammed began to laugh.

You've done it, haven't you? cried Mustafa. Didn't
I tell you to be careful or you'd get into trouble?

This is the way it had to be, or it wouldn't have

happened this way, Mohammed told him. I've done it, and I've got to keep her.

Mohammed, you're only a boy. Seventeen! You're going to ruin your life with an army of babies. In a little while the only thing you'll be good for is worrying. No more life, no fun, no nights with your friends. From the house to work. From work to house. The babies always sick. Something always wrong. Never any money. By the time you're thirty you'll be an old man, good for nothing. Like me. I'm twenty-seven. But I've got three, and I look sixty.

Just tell me if you know of a house, said Mohammed.

I think I can get one for you by the end of the week.

Where?

In Benider.

Mohammed had decided that during the next few days he would spend all his time with Mr. David, eating, drinking and sleeping with him, and going with him wherever he wanted him to go. It was a great pleasure for Mr. David when Mohammed would consent to go with him to a party.

The next morning at breakfast he mentioned the money. It's going to be expensive, he said. I should have stayed in jail.

Don't talk that way, said Mr. David. We'll manage.

20

THE NEXT DAY Mohammed met Mina's father in the
Zoco Chico, and they walked down to the tunnel that
led into the courtyard of the notaries. They went
through the gate. There was a basin full of goldfish in
the center, under some small orange trees. They sat
down on a bench and waited. Mohammed took out a
cigarette and began to smoke.

Finally they were taken into the notary's office.
What do you want?

Si Ahmed said: Sidi, this boy.

Let me talk to him, said Mohammed.

Talk, said Si Ahmed.

Sidi, an accident has happened between me and a
girl. She came to my house and spent the night, and I
damaged her. What we want is to arrange it so no one
will know anything about it. No one but Allah. I want
to make out the papers according to the law.

I must talk with the girl, said the notary. We can't
do anything unless she's here, too.

You can come to the house and see her, said Mohammed.

That will cost you more.

It's all right.

The notary got up and put his books and pens into a briefcase. Then he went out and found two assistants to go with him, and all five of them set out through the Medina to go to Mstakhoche.

When they got to Si Ahmed's house, Mina served them pastries and made them tea. Then she sat down facing the notary.

Mina, do you love this boy? he asked her.

Yes, Sidi, she said.

Not just think it would be fun to marry him, and then after three or four days decide you don't like him?

No, Sidi. I'll never, never leave him until the day I die.

Good, good, said the notary. Then he turned to Si Ahmed. How much are you asking for the girl?

A hundred thousand francs, said Si Ahmed.

You heard that? the notary asked Mohammed.

Yes, said Mohammed. A hundred thousand. It's all right. He was thinking about Mr. David. I'll have it here for you tomorrow.

21

MOHAMMED WAS SITTING in a beach chair in the garden outside Mr. David's room. He could hear him typing inside. When he would stop for a moment, Mohammed would cough. Soon Mr. David came to the door, and saw Mohammed leaning forward with his head in his hands. Mohammed, he said.

Mohammed did not look up.

Now what's the matter?

Finally Mohammed stood up. I came to say goodbye, he said. I've got to go back to jail.

Back to jail! cried Mr. David. I thought it was all arranged.

How can it be arranged if her father wants a hundred thousand francs for her? He's a criminal! I told him I'd go back to jail before I'd pay that much.

You will not! You'll pay him the money.

I have to pay him tomorrow. How can I?

Mr. David sighed. I told you I'd help you, he said. You can't go back to jail.

It's robbery, said Mohammed.

That day he stayed by Mr. David's side. He mixed

his drinks for him, and had a match ready each time he took out a cigarette. And when evening came, he helped him into his bathrobe, and listened with him to London on the radio, instead of switching the program to Rabat as he always did. Before they went to sleep Mr. David told him that he had never known another boy like him.

The next day Mohammed went back to Mstakhoche with the money in his pocket. The notary and his assistants were sitting in a row on the mattress, and Si Ahmed's face looked worried. It changed when Mohammed came in, walked over to the notary and counted out the money. The notary counted it again and handed it to Si Ahmed. Then Mohammed signed. When the notary himself had written his name on each paper, Mohammed gave him another ten thousand francs.

Keep this paper, the notary said. At the end of the month you have to take it to the qadi. You sign it in front of him, and he'll give you the final paper. Then it will all be in order.

Mohammed folded the paper and put it into his pocket. The notary and his assistants got up. Bslemah, bslemah, they said. May Allah give you happiness, they told Mina. And they went out.

22

SO, IT'S ALL settled, said Mina's mother. I hope
you'll both be very happy. Allah ikimil aleikoum
b'kheir.

Mina was not listening to her.

Her mother went on. We've got to begin to think
about the wedding party.

Let me tell you something, said Mina. You've just
sold me, haven't you? You couldn't have said to the
notary: I'll give her away according to the Koran. I
don't want any money for her. When you heard the
words: How much? you had to say: A hundred thousand francs. And this boy paid the hundred thousand.
He bought a girl. He's got the paper in his pocket.

Mina! cried her mother.

Mina turned to her.

He shouldn't have had to pay anything. It's shame-
ful what my father did! Does he think I'm a cow? He
sold me for a hundred thousand francs, and now he's
got the money. Is that right? So I'm not yours any
longer, and I'm not going to live here, and I don't
want any wedding party.

We're poor, said Si Ahmed. If we'd given you away for nothing, where would we have got the money for the wedding party? We haven't got enough.

You haven't got enough! I know what you have! Mina cried. You could pay for six weddings! You're just stingy. All you know how to do is get money out of people. You don't know how to let go of it, do you? You think everybody doesn't know what a miser you are? You can't think of anything else, even in your sleep. And I don't want any party.

Mohammed got up. I'm going. You're staying here, he said to Mina.

Mina did not reply. He said good-bye. He had promised to let Mr. David know what had happened with the notary.

Mr. David was waiting for him. Is it all right? he asked him.

Mohammed handed him the piece of paper the notary had given him.

It's all in Arabic, said Mr. David. What does it say?

It says I'm married to Mina.

Is that all they give you?

Why? What more should they give you?

Mr. David laughed. The Moslem world always made him laugh, because he knew nothing about it. Mohammed did not tell him that he had to go and see the qadi at the end of the month in order to get the final papers.

23

AT THE END of the week Mohammed saw Mustafa again, and they went to look at the house in Benider. Mustafa unlocked the door. There were two rooms, a kitchen and a bathroom.

It's not a bad place, said Mohammed.

There's a good terrace on the roof.

How much is it?

Three thousand. The owner gave it to me to rent for him. I could get more from somebody else.

Mohammed pulled out the money and gave it to Mustafa. I'm bringing my things tonight.

You've got two keys to the house, Mustafa told him, and he handed the keys to Mohammed as they went out into the street.

Mohammed hurried down to the Fondaq ech Chijra and hired a truck with two porters. He got in beside the driver and had him go to Mstakhoche. They carried everything out of the mahal and took it into the city, to the house in Benider. When it was all inside, he paid the men and they left.

He spent the whole afternoon arranging the furniture the way he wanted it. Then he went to the hotel. At first he thought he would tell Mr. David about the house, and take him to see it, because he was pleased with the way it looked. Then he decided not to say anything about it that day.

Now that the house was ready, he was eager to show it to Mina. The next morning he went to Mstakhoche and knocked on the door of her house. Mina herself came to answer. There's nobody home, she said. You can't come in.

Meet me in the garden at five, he said. I've got something to show you.

And in the afternoon he took her down to the house in Benider. As soon as she saw it she said: I'm moving in tonight.

Before the wedding? You can't. Your family'll make a scandal.

If I wait at home there'll never be any wedding, she said. My father's got the money now. That's all he cares about.

They'll blame me, said Mohammed.

They don't care now, as long as nobody knows about it. But if I come and stay here, it'll worry them and they'll want to get the wedding over with.

Tomorrow's better, he told her.

24

MOHAMMED SLEPT WITH Mr. David that night. The next morning early he was at the house in Benider, waiting for Mina to arrive. She came about ten o'clock with all her clothes.

What did they say? he wanted to know.

She shrugged. Nothing very much. Only they're going to have the wedding party soon.

Good, said Mohammed. Now let's go out. I want us to have our picture taken, so we'll have a souvenir of today. If anything should happen to either one of us, at least the other would have a souvenir.

Yes, that's true. She put on a woollen skirt and a white blouse and an open sweater. Her hair fell to her shoulders and then curved outwards. He combed it for her until it looked the way he wanted it to look. Then they set out for Emsallah. There was a photographer's studio there with a sign that said: CASA LUX. They went in.

Qué quieren?

Queremos hacer una foto, said Mohammed. We

want the largest size, and with the widest frame. How much will it cost?

The proprietor said: I can make it for you for seven thousand francs, with the coloring and the glass.

Yes, said Mohammed. The Spaniard took them inside, into a room where there was a big screen with trees painted across it. He put two chairs side by side. Then he told them to sit down facing him. Mina put one arm around Mohammed, and he put one arm around her. The Spaniard uncovered his machine and took the photograph. Mohammed gave him two thousand francs on account, put the receipt into his pocket, and took Mina out into the street. They walked down through Emsallah and stopped in front of a shop that sold kitchen utensils.

We need all sorts of things, Mohammed said. They bought as many things as they were able to carry between them, and took a taxi back to the Medina.

Mohammed wanted to get a woman to help clean the house, but Mina thought they should do it themselves. They spent the afternoon working there together. When it got dark, he said to her: Let's eat dinner and go to the cinema.

They went into the kitchen. Mina put a pot on the stove and poured some oil into it. Mohammed sat down and began to peel potatoes. They finally got the meal ready. It was not very good and they ate it quickly. Then Mohammed went back into the kitchen and made coffee while Mina was changing.

25

THEY WALKED SLOWLY up the Boulevard. When they got to the Ciné Roxy they looked at the photos outside. It was a film of Brigitte Bardot. They went in and sat down.

Mina began to whisper: What a pretty girl she is!

I'm not interested in Brigitte Bardot or any of the others, he told her. I've got something here with me better than a hundred Brigitte Bardots, and that's all I want. There's nobody like you. You're different from all the others. That's what scares me. I'm afraid somebody's going to take you away from me.

Oh, no! she exclaimed. Why do you say that?

They might, he said. He could not give her the true reason: that he knew she could never have real love for him because the false love of the spell had taken its place, and that the effect of the magic could end at any time.

He went on. When I walk with you in the street, people look at us and think: Look at that beautiful girl. Like a rose. And what a perfect body!

Mohammed!

How could anyone compare Brigitte Bardot to you? Next to you she looks like nothing. Nothing at all.

Thank you, Mohammed, she said. When I'm sitting alone at home, I think of you. I can see you right there, standing in front of me. And I say to myself: How can any boy be so handsome? And so strong? And so sweet-natured and good-hearted too? Nobody can make me feel the way he does. He's more beautiful than I am. And then you disappear.

Only girls are beautiful, said Mohammed. Let's watch Brigitte Bardot now.

He put his arm around her and kissed her eyelids and her cheeks and her lips. Then he began to kiss her throat. He unbuttoned her blouse.

There are people behind us, she whispered.

They sat through to the end of Brigitte Bardot, and then they went out.

Let's go and sit in a café, he said.

All right.

They walked over to the Café Pilo and went inside.

He called a waiter. Bring us two orders of chicken with some peas on the side. And a Coca-Cola and a beer.

The food was put on the table, and Mohammed said: Eat.

They ate and drank. He kept ordering more beer.

When they went out of the café he had his arm around her, and he rolled from side to side as he walked. He held her head under his arm as they went down the hill past the Hotel Minzah, and he was singing.

Don't sing! she kept telling him. If a policeman comes along, he's going to take us to the comisaría.

What's the comisaría? he cried. I never heard of it. Keep going, and don't talk so much.

All the way down the hill he stopped every few seconds and took her face between his hands to kiss it. You're the most beautiful girl in the world, he would tell her. Or: You're my whole life. Or: Nobody ever existed that I could love the way I love you.

They got to the house and went in. Then he took her in his arms. He picked her up, carried her to the bed, and laid her carefully down on the soft mattress. She laughed and jumped up.

He took off his jacket and hung it on a chair. He took off his shirt and his shoes and his socks and his trousers. Mina came out of the bathroom wearing one of the nightgowns he had bought her. It was made of very thin material. He turned off the lights, and left only a little lamp on the night table. It gave a very dim green light. They got into bed and began to kiss.

I love you! I love you! Mohammed cried.

One person doesn't love another person, she told him. It's not the person that loves. It's the heart. My heart loves your heart, Mohammed. And I wish I knew why.

Don't think about it, he said. They kissed and held one another very close.

Mohammed turned off the green light, and they went to sleep.

26

MINA STAYED ON at the house in Benider with Mohammed. Time went by. Her parents did not come to see her, and she began to worry. One morning she said to Mohammed: I've got to go and find out what's happening. Are they getting ready for the wedding or not?

She came back pleased, and said that the wedding would take place soon. Several times during the next few days she went to see her mother, and she became more and more excited.

Thinking about Mina's party was making Mohammed unhappy about not being able to have his own. He decided that if only one party were going to be given, he was going to be there. No man ever goes into a girl's wedding party. However, he thought his plan would work.

One day not long afterwards Si Ahmed went down to the town and bought a young bull and two sacks of flour. He got two men to lead the bull and carry the flour back to Mstakhoche. A great many women had come to the house to help Mina's mother knead the dough for the fqaqas. They had hired a black woman to go around from house to house announcing the wedding and inviting the women to come to it, and Si Ahmed had sent to Tetuan for Andaluz musicians.

The hotel was full of tourists. Mohammed stood behind the bar talking with Mr. David. I'm inviting you now to my wedding party, he told him. I'll let you know when it's going to be. You've got to come.

Mr. David was delighted. Thank you, Mohammed. A real Arab wedding? I'll certainly be there.

And bring whoever you like, said Mohammed. Bring lots of people. The only thing is that everybody must wear evening clothes, and each one brings a present of some sort with him. As you go through the door you hand the present to Mina's mother. That's the custom.

I understand, said Mr. David.

That night and the others that followed, Mr. David told several American and English people about the great chance they soon would have of going with him to a native wedding ceremony. When the day was finally set for the party, Mohammed gave him the news, and he began telephoning to tell his friends where he would meet them in order to take them out to Mstakhoche.

Remember, you've got to have some sort of gift with you, he told each one, and they all agreed.

The night of the party came. The house was full of girls and women in their best kaftans, and they were all dancing. Mina sat on cushions without moving, and everyone passed by her to admire her. She was wearing a white European-style wedding gown.

Mohammed and his friends drove out in three cars. There were nine of them, and they all wore dinner jackets. They walked in a group to Mina's house, and Mohammed knocked on the door. When Mina's mother opened it and saw Mohammed, she was very angry. What are you doing here? she cried.

Mohammed bowed. Lalla Khaddouj, these Nazarenes wanted to come with their presents for Mina.

Nazarenes? she said. Then she saw all the Europeans standing there holding their packages wrapped in tissue paper and tied with ribbons. Wait, she told Mohammed. She shut the door and went in to talk with the other women of the family. Mohammed heard them saying: They don't know any better. We can hide them. You'll have to let them in.

After a while Mina's mother came back to the door and threw it open.

They can come in, she said. Their room is in there. She pointed to one end of a room where they had hung sheets. The Europeans handed their gifts to Mina's mother, and went through the room to sit down on the mattresses behind the sheets.

It's like being in a tent. You can't see anything! the Nazarenes kept saying.

This is the way they do it, Mr. David explained.

They drank tea and ate couscous and pastries.

Some of the Europeans had kif with them, and smoked it, and pounded on the trays in rhythm with the music.

This is a modern wedding, Mohammed told them. Instead of waiting at home for the bride, I've come myself to get her. That's the way it ought to be done.

About midnight the music stopped. Mohammed jumped up. We've got to leave now, he told them.

They all went out into the street. The women and girls were calling: Youyouyouyou! Mina kissed her mother good-bye, and walked with Mohammed to the place where the cars were parked. Everyone else walked behind.

Mr. David drove Mohammed and Mina in the Mercedes, and the other cars followed. There were eight taxis full of Moslems. They went directly to the Casa Lux studio, where Mohammed had arranged with the Spaniard to keep the place open until they arrived.

Mohammed and Mina went in and sat for their picture, and as they came out the girls and women began once more to scream: Youyouyouyou! After that they set out for the Boulevard Pasteur to drive up and down and blow their horns for an hour or so. Everyone who could reach was pounding on the sides of the cars. The ones inside clapped their hands and played drums. They sang: Aabaha, aabaha, ouallah makhallaha! When they had finished on the Boulevard they drove down to the waterfront and parked the cars at the bottom of the Ciné Americano stairway. They climbed the stairs and went singing and laughing through the alleys to the house in Benider.

Some of the guests sat on the mattresses drinking Coca-Cola and eating pastries. Mohammed stayed with the Europeans in the other room. Mr. David had hidden several bottles of whisky in the car, to drink after they left Mina's house, because Mohammed had told him not to take alcohol to the wedding party. After a long while, they said it was time to go.

Mina and Mohammed stood alone in the doorway looking after them.

27

MOHAMMED SHUT THE door.

You see? he said. All the things you were afraid of, that people would talk about you, that your father was going to beat you, that I wasn't really going to marry you, all those things were in your head. Everybody's happy. Your family, your friends. And so are we.

They kissed each other. Mohammed went into the kitchen. He lighted the stove and made some coffee. Then he put some pastries on a plate.

Why didn't you let me make the coffee? Mina said.

I don't want those little hands to do anything, he told her. And he cut the pastry into pieces and pushed them into her mouth. Then he held up her cup of coffee to her lips and tried to make her drink it. She could not do it very well. He pulled out his handkerchief and wiped her mouth and chin.

From now on, he said, I'm going to get up in the morning and make breakfast. Then I'll bring it in here to you and you can eat it in bed. And I'll feed you and wash your face.

No, she said. I married you to help you. I'm going

to wash your clothes and iron them and mend them. And I'm going to cook for you.

Let's go to bed, said Mohammed. They took off their clothes and got into bed. He held her in his arms.

Now you're really my wife, he told her. Up to now we've had a marriage like the wind, like false money. But now we have a real one. And he kissed her. The day I have a son, he went on, I'm going to invite everybody in Tangier to a party, Moslems and Nazarenes, and I'm going to have an orchestra.

Incha'Allah, murmured Mina.

He looked closely at her. Mina, there's something on your mind. Tell me. What are you worried about?

My mother, she said.

Your mother! Why?

Mohammed, she doesn't like you. She's going to do something. For years she's been planning to have me marry her brother-in-law's nephew. But I'd never have married him.

You didn't tell me.

I know, but it's true.

Mohammed said: Your mother's not going to do anything. After all we've gone through so we could be together, are we going to let her break us up? Stop thinking about your mother. What can she do if we love each other?

I suppose you're right, said Mina.

They went back to kissing and hugging, and played games together for a long time. Finally Mohammed turned out the light and they went to sleep.

28

A LOUD KNOCKING at the door awoke them in the middle of the morning. Mina got up, put on her bathrobe, and went to open the door. The street was full of women and girls, and they were singing and laughing. Her family and friends had come to pay the visit of the morning after the wedding. They pushed into the house.

Mina frowned. It's too early, she told them. My husband is still asleep.

When they heard this, they all began to scream: Youyouyouyou! and to clap their hands. Many of the girls had brought drums with them. They pulled them out and pounded on them.

With all the noise, Mohammed woke up. He ran into the bathroom and slammed the door. There he washed and dressed quickly. Then he put on his bridegroom's slippers, and without looking towards the women and girls, he hurried to the door and went out into the street. He did not want to lose his new white slippers so soon. If the girls had been able to catch him, they would all have rushed at him and pulled them from his feet. He went down to the Zoco Chico and sat in the sun on the terrace of the Café Central.

Soon he saw some of his friends going past. He called to them.

Sit down, he told them.

I hear you're married, said Ali.

That's right.

Wait until she begins filling up with brats. You won't even be able to buy yourself a new pair of shoes. You'll be going along in the street barefoot and you won't even know it.

Mohammed did not want to listen. I've got to get some breakfast, he said. He got up and went around the corner into the Calle del Comercio. There was a stall there with tubes of flickering light in the ceiling. He sat down at a table. When he had eaten he remained sitting there, looking into the street, watching people walk by. Time passed slowly, but there was no way of going home while the women were still there.

29

IN THE WEEKS, and finally the months, that followed, Mr. David grew more and more nervous. It seemed to him that Mohammed was taking a long time to get rid of Mina. He came to the hotel to see him several times a week, but it was always in the afternoon, and Mr. David preferred to see him at night.

If you don't leave her soon, she'll be having a baby, he would tell Mohammed. Then you'll be in a cage.

Mohammed would look at him with an empty face and say: Yes. Mr. David suspected that he did not intend to separate from Mina, and this made him angry. Sometimes Mohammed was surprised by the unfriendliness he saw in Mr. David's face.

Often when Mohammed went to the hotel Mina would go to see her mother. As time passed, she went more and more frequently, until she was spending some part of nearly every day in Mstakhoche. Mohammed thought about this and was troubled by it. It seemed to him a bad idea that she should pass so much time with someone who probably did not like him. Each time he thought about it he was more certain that Lalla Khaddouj spoke ill of him to Mina. When she came back from there he would watch her carefully for some sign that would prove he was right.

It was winter now. The markets were full of flowers and people's clothes were always wet with rain. Mohammed drank only whisky these days, but he drank a great deal of it, and many times came home very drunk.

One evening when he arrived at the house in Benider he opened the door and stood a moment with his hand on the wall to steady himself. Mina was looking at him. He shut the door and walked across the room to kiss her, but she turned her head away.

Why are you doing that? What am I, garbage or something?

No. Did you ever take that paper to the qadi?

He was surprised to see that she remembered it. No, he said, I haven't had a chance. I've been too busy.

Mina walked away and went into the kitchen.

Another night when he got home she was not there. She came in soon afterwards, and looked at Mohammed without speaking to him. He watched her changing her clothes. When she had finished, he said: Where have you been? To your mother's?

She turned angrily towards him. Where else would I have been?

What's the matter with you? What's happened?

Leave me alone! she shouted. Go out for a walk.

Or go and sit with your friends. Just leave me alone.

What are you so excited about? You don't have to yell.

Don't talk to me.

All right. He went out into the other room and sat down on the couch.

When Mina had prepared supper, she brought in food for him, and none for herself.

Come here and eat, he told her.

No. I don't want to eat. I'm not hungry.

He got up from the table, put on his jacket, and went out into the street. At the Café Fuentes he sat down and ordered black coffee. He looked at the floor under his feet, wondering what had happened. It was possible that Mina's mother had gone to consult a fqih who had discovered the spell. If that were the case, they were already working to destroy the effect of it. Or it could merely be her mother's talking against him day after day.

He paid for the coffee and went home. Mina was in bed asleep. He put on his pyjamas and got into bed beside her. When he tried to play with her and kiss her, he had the feeling that she had become somebody else. In the end she kissed him, but not in the way she always had until now. Something was missing. For the first time, they lay together, and did not make love, and the night was like a poison to Mohammed.

30

THE NEXT DAY Mohammed said to Mr. David: I'd like to sleep here with you tonight.

It made him feel good to see Mr. David happy. That night Mr. David did not mention Mina at all, nor the next night, nor the next night. Mohammed spent three nights, one after the other, with Mr. David, going back to the house in Benider each day at sunrise, when Mina returned from her mother's. She would come in and be busy around the house, but she spoke to him only if he asked her a question.

The fourth night he decided to sleep in the house. As soon as he got into bed she turned over, saying she felt sick. Mohammed slept very badly.

The next morning Mina was up very early.

What's the matter? said Mohammed.

I've got to spend the whole day at my mother's, she said.

At home in Mstakhoche Mina found an old woman sitting with her mother.

Mina! cried her mother. Come and have Lalla Meriam tell your fortune. She throws snails onto the dirt. She's just told mine. Sit down and let her tell yours.

Mina sat down and the woman began to look carefully at her. She had a black cloth spread out, and it was covered with sand. She shook the snails back and forth in her fist, and then tossed them out onto the sand.

My daughter, she told Mina, you're under a spell. And the one who put it on you is a boy. He's not tall, and he's not short either. Medium. And he's still very young. He wants you all for himself. You think you like him, but you don't like him at all. It's just the magic working.

Mina looked at her with wide eyes. The woman nodded her head slowly, up and down.

Can't you help her? cried Mina's mother.

Yes. I can get her out of it. But it's expensive work.

How much?

It comes to around fifteen thousand francs. But I can cure her.

It's worth it, said Mina's mother. I'll pay for it. I can get the money.

Good, said Lalla Meriam.

Do you agree? her mother asked Mina.

Mina was thinking of Mohammed, and how he would come into the house and fall onto the bed, smelling of what he had drunk.

Yes, she said.

31

THAT EVENING MOHAMMED came in and went to kiss Mina, but it was like kissing the wall.

Ouakha, he said to himself. That night they lay in bed listening to the rain. They did not touch one another.

In the morning Mohammed went out without breakfast. Mina was still asleep. He walked to the courtyard of the notaries. He had the paper in his pocket, and he was going to tell the notary that he had changed his mind. I don't want the girl, he said to himself as he walked along. I'm going to get rid of her. Then he thought: That means she'll get everything in the house.

He stopped as he came to the doorway. Why, he asked himself. Why should I lose everything? There's the money hidden there, and all the jewelry I bought her. She'll marry somebody else and he'll get it all. Or when she's stayed her forty days she won't give back the key. No! I'll put up with it and see what happens. If I play a good game I'll win. I'll keep everything, and she'll go out of the house with her hands folded over her heart, without money, without furniture, without clothes.

He turned around and went back into the street.

Now he slept every night with Mr. David. Each morning he would get up, take a kouffa and go to the market to buy Mina her food for the day. Then he would carry it to the house in Benider and leave it with her. She never seemed glad to see him. Once in a while, when her face was a little less angry, he would return at night, hoping to stay. But he never did.

One morning when he came in she began to complain. There's nothing to eat in the house! she cried. I want some bananas. And get me some chocolates and some apples.

Mohammed stood still and looked at her. This is bad, he thought. She's got a baby inside her. And then he thought: It's mine, and he felt very happy.

That morning, and the mornings afterwards, he went out and searched in the different markets for chirimoyas, grapes, tangerines, and every other kind of fruit he could find. And he brought her chocolates and biscuits. He did not even mind her bad humor, or care when she found fault with everything he brought her. He would sit and watch her eat it, and then comfort her when she vomited it up.

Mina's mother now forbade her to visit her in Mstakhoche, saying it would be bad for her health to go into the street. She came to the city each day to see her. Mohammed knew that, but he did not know that each day she stopped on the way at Lalla Meriam's

house to get a fresh batch of the powder the old
woman was making in order to cure Mina.

As soon as she got to the house in Benider, Mina's
mother would sprinkle the powder over the coals of
the brazier. She always arrived in the afternoon when
Mohammed was not there. She had arranged a system
of signals with Mina, and if he happened to be in the
house, she would wait hidden in a stall or a doorway
until she saw him go out. Then quickly she would run
to the door and knock. And Mina would have the
coals ready in the brazier.

Now Mohammed came more often to sleep. He arranged himself a bed on the mattress that lay along
the wall, in the bedroom with Mina. It excited him to
think that she was lying over there in the bed with his
baby inside her.

One night he awoke and heard her groaning. He
got up and went over to her.

I have a headache, she told him. He got her an
aspirin. Then she asked for a glass of coffee. When he
had got back into bed and turned off the light, she
called to him again.

I have a fever!

He brought her a basin of cold water and a cloth,
made a compress, and put it on her head. Now and
then he wrung it out. He was still sitting there by her
at seven in the morning. Then he went out to a pharmacy and told the clerk that his wife had a fever and a
headache.

The pharmacist gave him some pills and told him to

cover her well and let her sleep. He did as he had been told, and sat down again beside her, thinking of how his life had changed since Mina had stopped loving him. He was certain that her mother had something to do with it. She was determined to bring their love to an end. The thought frightened him. Suddenly he got up. He bent over Mina and kissed her lips.

32

ABOUT ELEVEN O'CLOCK Mina stirred and opened her eyes.

How are you? he said.

I feel fine.

She got up. While she was washing he stood in the kitchen having his breakfast. Then he went to the market and bought liver and beefsteak and salad. He took it back to the house and spent an hour or so preparing lunch. When it was ready they sat down. It was the first meal they had had together in half a month.

Tell me the truth, Mohammed said suddenly. Why don't you love me? What's happened?

Why do you say that? That I don't love you. Mina sighed. It's not true.

You're hiding something. You don't want to tell me.

She looked at him. Mohammed, if you did it, it's a sin. My mother says you put a spell on me. You liked me, and just because I didn't like you, you went out and paid somebody to put a spell on me. That's not love.

Mohammed tried to speak, but she would not let him.

A friend of my mother's found out. She says it's magic. And my mother's doing everything she can to break it, if it is. That's all I can tell you.

Your mother's an old bitch, said Mohammed.

I won't let you insult my mother! Mina cried. The fortune teller asked to see me. As soon as she saw me she said I was under a spell. And then she told me the whole thing.

What's finished is finished, said Mohammed. Anyway, he went on bitterly, I can see that whatever magic there was, your mother's already broken it.

It could be, said Mina thoughtfully. Mohammed's heart sank.

But we can stay together anyway, he said after a moment.

I wonder, said Mina. Every day you seem more like a stranger.

He got up and went out, down to the hotel, and into the back garden where Mr. David was sitting. Mr. David looked up.

What's the matter now?

Nothing.

Have a drink.

No. He sat in the hotel all day, looking sad. When night came he went back to the house. Mina was asleep in her bed. He climbed into his own bed, but he could not sleep. He got up and sat in a chair, smoking one cigarette after another. It's over, he thought. No more kisses and games and laughing, when we did whatever we wanted, and then when we were tired, fell asleep in each other's arms, my face against her face. These days when I come in she's there already asleep. If I climb into the bed with her she turns her back. If I touch her she hits me with her elbow. And when I finally get to her, I might as well be in the Moujahiddine with a corpse. What good is that?

He got up and went over to the bed. He pulled the sheet away from her face, bent over and kissed her. She did not stir. He knew she was awake. He put on his clothes quickly and went out to the Café Pilo to drink vodka. It was five in the morning. When he left the Café Pilo it was noon.

33

MOHAMMED GOT BACK to the house about half past one, very drunk. He opened the door and leaned inside. Mina saw him and came running to push against the door.

You can't come in! she cried. I won't have you in here like that.

He raised his arm to hit her. Then he lowered it.

You say that to me and you're not ashamed? He pushed her and went inside. Mina shut the door. Mohammed turned and tried to kiss her. She hit him in the mouth with the back of her hand, and her ring cut his lip. The blood dripped from his chin. He seized her.

I'd like to kill you now, he told her. And kill the one who's inside you. But I suppose it would be a sin. Since the day I was born, no woman or whore or girl has ever hit me, until you hit me now. You're living here in my house with me, eating my food. I've given you everything I have. You're living better than a sultana. You've got better clothes than you ever had in your life. What are you, anyway? You're just a Djiblia. Your father with his djellaba and his pants a kilometer wide, and the turban down over his ears like somebody in the cinema. I've made you into something civilized. I ought to have knocked you down when I came in, but I was sorry for you. And so you hit me.

Mina said nothing. She was merely looking at him. It made him happy to see that there was fear in her eyes. He walked out into the kitchen. There were some bottles of wine on the table. He took one and opened it. Mina had followed him and was standing by the door.

Mohammed sat down at the table and put his feet up on it. Sit down, he told her.

I'm going to ask you something, Mina. Do you want to go on with me or not? You know when I was supposed to be at the qadi's to sign the papers? Four months ago. More than four months. You understand?

Yes.

I never went back. Because when you cooled off I decided it wasn't worth it. But I'd like to know. Do you want to stay on and be my wife or don't you? I can go and sign the papers any time. If there's somebody else you want to go and live with, and he loves you and you love him, just say: Excuse me, Mohammed, I'm going. I won't stop you.

I'll think about it, she said.

He got up, lurched into the other room, and fell onto the bed. Drunk and dressed in his clothes, he went to sleep.

34

SOON MINA'S MOTHER arrived. She pulled out the brazier and poured her packet of powder over the coals, and the smoke filled the house. Mohammed did not stop sleeping. Lalla Khaddouj finished her work quietly, took up her kouffa, kissed Mina, and went out.

Late in the afternoon Mohammed woke up. He called out: Mina!

What is it?

What's that smell?

I put a little bakhour on the brazier.

That's not bakhour, he said. Bakhour never stank like that.

I mixed it, she said. I put in a little djaoui and some fasoukh.

I see. Who's been here?

Nobody.

Nobody came?

No.

Do you want to go to the cinema?

You know I can't go out, she said. Can't you see my belly? Are you making fun of me?

Lots of men take wives everywhere with their bellies sticking out. Europeans, Moslems. It's nothing.

I'd be too ashamed. I can't go out.

Ouakha, he said.

He went to the kitchen and spread some jam on a piece of bread. While he ate it he made some coffee. Then he went back into the other room and took hold of Mina. She grew stiff. He managed to kiss her in spite of her struggle. Then he went out.

A month or two went by. Most nights Mohammed slept with Mr. David at the hotel. But now and then he would begin to think about Mina, and the idea always came to him that someone else might be around. Then he would go and spend a night in the house at Benider.

35

ONE NIGHT WHEN Mohammed was there asleep on his mattress, Mina began to cry out: Ay, yimma! Ay, yimma!

What's the matter? he said.

My belly!

Mohammed got up and dressed. I must find a taxi first, he thought. It may be the baby.

He ran down to the Zoco Chico in the rain. After midnight the police allowed the taxis to line up there. He found one, and told the driver to wait. Then he went back to the house and wrapped Mina in a sheet, lifted her in his arms, and carried her groaning down through the alleys to the Zoco Chico where the taxi was waiting.

They went to the Spanish Hospital at Ain Qtiouat. Mohammed rang the bell. A guard came to the door. Two nurses carried Mina inside. After a while a doctor came and told Mohammed that his wife was fine, and that he could go home and sleep, and come back in the morning.

How can I go home and sleep? cried Mohammed.

He took a taxi that was waiting under the pine trees in front of the hospital and went back to the city. The streets were wet and empty. In the house at Benider he sat down in a chair and looked around the room. It was very still. He felt his flesh prickle. There was a sound inside his head as if someone were screaming. The fear came up from inside him. He rose and went into the kitchen.

He lighted the stove and made a glass of strong black coffee. He sat down at the kitchen table and listened to the rain running down the drainpipe. He lit a cigarette and watched his hand tremble. Quickly he finished the coffee and went out into the street. He did not want to see the house or think about it.

In the Zoco Chico the water was running down the middle of the sidewalk. He sat under the awning at the Café Fuentes and ordered a black coffee. At seven in the morning he stood up and paid for the coffees he had drunk. Then he took a taxi to the hospital.

They led him up to the room where Mina was, and he found her lying in bed with the baby beside her. Her eyes were shut. When he touched her she opened them, and he kissed her. They both laughed. He took the baby in his arms. It was a boy. He tried to tickle him, but the baby screamed.

What are we going to call him? said Mina.

Driss, we'll call him.

Ouakha, she said. It's a pretty name.

You won't be in here long, he told her. You'll be

home soon. We'll have a big party and invite everybody. We'll have hundreds of pastries.

Incha'Allah.

He kissed her. Get well. Good-bye.

He went down to the hotel and told Mr. David about the baby. Then he said: I'm going in to bed.

Now? Why?

I couldn't stay alone in the house, so I sat in the café.

So now she's got the baby, said Mr. David. I told you from the beginning if you got married you'd have a terrible life. You can have any girl you want. You didn't have to marry her. I could have got you out of that. But you wanted to marry her, that's the truth. And now look at you. Are you happy?

No matter how much you'd paid for your lawyers you couldn't have done anything for me, said Mohammed. What I did was a crime. There's no way of getting off on that charge. Anyway, it's all happened, and I'm tired. I've got to go and sleep.

Go to the studio, said Mr. David. It's quieter in there.

Mohammed went to the room, shut the door behind him, and dropped onto the couch.

A person dressed all in white was coming towards him. It was saying: May you always be in good health, Mohammed. Allah has preserved you from many evil things. Soon you will have a new life.

When he got up it was seven in the evening. He

shaved and went into the bar. He made himself a glass of coffee. Mr. David was sitting with some Englishmen. Mohammed told him his dream.

It sounds like a good dream, said Mr. David. It might have been one of your Moslem saints come to talk with you.

Mr. David did not know anything about Moslem saints. Mohammed went on drinking his coffee.

36

WHEN MINA WAS out of the hospital and back at the house in Benider, she stayed in bed the first day. Mohammed sat in the chair facing her. Now and then he would tell her again how glad he was to see her at home. At last I'll be able to sleep, he said.

Where have you been sleeping these two nights? she asked him.

I couldn't sleep here alone, he said. I had a noise in my head. I had to go and sleep in the hotel.

She laughed. What were you afraid of?

I don't know. The night I came back I had gooseflesh.

And now? How do you feel?

Now? I'm happy. The baby's beautiful. And when he gets his name he'll be even more beautiful. And we'll have the party here.

Why don't we have it at my mother's house? said Mina.

He did not answer at first. I don't know what to say, he told her.

What do you mean?

I want it here. I want my friends to come. The baby was born on Saturday. Next Saturday we'll have a party.

On Thursday he went to the souq at Souani and bought two large rams. And he bought oil and white flour and almonds and raisins and onions to go with their flesh. When he got back to the house he found Mina's mother and her older sisters and several women neighbors already starting to make the pastries. They were going to try a special kind called Qadi's Turbans.

On Saturday Mohammed went to see a fqih in the quarter and asked him to go with him back to the house. There he led him up onto the roof where Mina stood with the baby in her arms, along with the other women who were holding the rams.

The fqih seized one of the rams by its horns, and Mohammed took hold of its body. Bismillah! Allah o akbar ala Driss! the fqih cried. He ran the knife once across its neck, and the animal fell. Mohammed had set a glass nearby. Quickly he put it beside the sheep's neck and filled it with the blood that was coming out. While the ram was still living he drank it. The women screamed: Youyouyouyou! as he wiped the blood from his lips. Soon they sacrificed the other ram, so there would be enough meat for all the guests. The Sudanese slave-woman that Mohammed had hired to wait on the party pounded on the door, and they went down and let her in. On the roof the women were stripping the hides from the carcasses and cutting flesh into pieces. Then they soaked the flesh in pots of cold water and put it to cook.

Mohammed went all around the town inviting his American and English friends to the feast. He had arranged the bedroom as the place where the Nazarenes would sit together, and one end of the sala was blanketed off from the rest. The Moslem women would be behind the blanket. In the Nazarene room he had a bottle of whisky, a bottle of gin, a bottle of vodka, a pail of ice, and soda and tonic water. In the room for the women he put a brazier with a teapot on it, and silver boxes of mint and verbena and orange buds.

Several days earlier he had asked a Djibli musician he knew to bring his orchestra and dancing boys. They arrived before the other guests, and the boys got into their girls' clothing, to be ready to dance. In their velvet kaftans and their gauze tfins and their sashes they looked better than girls. When the guests arrived the boys got up and began to dance. On their heads they carried trays full of tea glasses and lighted candles. The musicians were singing and playing their drums and violins and lutes and tambourines, and the boys were whirling around among the guests. The Americans clapped their hands very loud and began to shout. While they were eating they kept telling Mohammed how much they liked the food. They emptied all the bottles on the taifor and began to dance, trying to do the same steps as the Djibli boys.

When the Moslems saw the Nazarenes having such a good time, they decided it was a fine party, and they too enjoyed themselves.

At three o'clock in the morning the musicians stopped playing and said good night. Then the other people got their coats and wraps and went out. And Mohammed and Mina were left alone.

Everybody had a good time, he said. Hamdoul'lah!

Yes.

Are you happy?

Of course, she said.

Because of the baby. Isn't that why?

No. Not just the baby, she said. You too.

He laughed scornfully. Yes. I know how happy I make you.

They got ready for bed. Mina put the baby into its crib. It had been lying on the couch so everyone could see it.

She got into bed. He kissed her, and went to his bed.

Just before daybreak he awoke. He could hear Mina's soft breathing. He got up, went over to the bed, and slipped in beside her. When he kissed her, she pushed him away and said: Leave me alone. I'm sleepy.

You can sleep whenever you like, he told her. You've got all day and all night.

No! Let me sleep.

But he held her tight and went on kissing her. She was not yet well from the birth seven days before, and she made it difficult for him to have her. He knew he would not be able to sleep again until he had done what he wanted, and he kept on struggling with her until he had won the battle. Then he went back to his bed and quickly fell asleep.

37

AT ELEVEN O'CLOCK in the morning Mohammed was up, bathing. When Mina appeared, she was angry. Don't you ever do that again, she said. Coming and waking me up in the middle of the night and bothering me.

It's not my fault, said Mohammed. I can't help it. I can't sleep. When I feel like doing something, with you or anybody else, I have to do it. It's a habit of mine.

I don't like your habit, she told him.

What are you complaining about? You're still whole. Nothing so awful happened to you. I didn't eat you.

Finally she laughed. Then she said: I'm going out to my mother's.

Ouakha. There's money on the table for the taxi.

Mina took the baby and went off to her mother's house in Mstakhoche. Lalla Meriam was sitting there with Mina's mother.

Very good! Very good! cried Lalla Meriam. Your daughter has come just at the right moment.

I was only now talking to your mother, she said to Mina. I have some new things I want you to take home and try on your brazier. This powder I'm giving to your mother. She'll go with you to your house and put it on the fire for you. Then you must straddle the brazier and let the smoke go up. If the power explodes under you, you'll know once and for all that Mohammed gave you magic, and that it's broken. Everything will be all right then for you. If it doesn't explode, you'll know the whole thing was nothing anyway, a love as empty as air. And you won't have to worry any more in either case.

Later that day Mina and her mother went back to the house in Benider and did as Lalla Meriam had told them. And while Mina was straddling the brazier and feeling the heat of the coals all the way up to her belly, there was a loud cracking sound below her, and she screamed.

Hamdoul'lah! Allah has saved you! her mother cried. You're safe. The spell is broken. Now at last you're going to be happy.

I hope so, said Mina. Why don't you sit down now? I'll make you a glass of tea.

They sat down and talked, and drank their tea. At last her mother said: I've got to go. I did what I said I'd do. You're free now.

She kissed Mina and went out.

38

MR. DAVID WAS getting ready to make a trip with some American friends, and he mentioned it at lunch one day.

Would you be able to go with us? he asked Mohammed. He felt certain that Mohammed was going to refuse. We're going to Spain to look around and buy some clothes.

I'll go with you, said Mohammed. I'll have to let Mina know.

We're going tomorrow on the afternoon ferry, said Mr. David, looking very happy. It leaves at three-thirty.

Mohammed went home. Mina, he said. I have something to tell you, but don't get angry.

Why should I get angry? What is it?

Mr. David has to go to Spain, and I'm going with him. We'll be over there a week or ten days. If you don't want to stay here alone, why don't you sleep at your mother's? Or have her come here.

Ouakha, she said.

He gave her some money, took what clothes he

needed, and kissed her good-bye. And he lifted up the baby and kissed it, so that it began to cry.

Allah ihennik.

He went back to the hotel and went on packing his bags, putting in the things that he kept at Mr. David's. In the morning he went up to the Spanish Consulate and got his visa. The Americans invited him to have lunch with them in the bar. Then the four of them got into the Mercedes with their luggage and drove to the port.

In Madrid the Americans took Mohammed to bars and dance halls and night clubs, but he did not seem to be enjoying himself. He was sad and had nothing to say. Much of the time he was thinking about Mina's mother. She may try to do something now that I'm not there, he thought.

The ten days finally passed, and Mohammed never brightened. He bought a great many presents for Mina and Driss, and when they came back into Tangier he got them all through the customs without paying duty. Mr. David let him take the Volkswagen to carry the packages home.

At the house in Benider, carrying his luggage and the bundles, he began to knock on the door.

Ah, Hamdoul'lah! Mina cried when she saw him. How are you, Mohammed?

He kissed her and went into the house.

What did you bring me from Spain?

All these parcels here are for you, he told her.

She unwrapped six or seven dresses and four pairs of shoes and three handbags. There were baby clothes, and several bottles of perfume and jars of powder and tubes of cream.

So many things! she kept saying. Thank you!

It's nothing.

She went into the other room and tried on one of the dresses. How's this one? she wanted to know, walking back and forth.

Beautiful, he said.

She quickly put on another. And this one? she asked him. Do you like this one?

Even better than the other.

She tried all the dresses and bags and shoes. And he said: Yes, yes, to everything, because she looked more beautiful than ever before.

He went over to the crib and lifted the baby out of it. He poked it and kissed it, and asked it when it was going to be big, so it could go out for walks with him and he could take it to the cinema and the beach. And school, he said. You've got to go to school. And maybe you'll be a fqih, or a doctor, or a lawyer, or a minister in the government. Something important. Not like me.

I'm going to my mother's now, Mina said.

But I just got back, and I want to lie down for a little while. You can go later. Or tomorrow.

No. I can't. I have to go now.

I see, said Mohammed. Well, you know the way.

She took the baby and went out, and Mohammed lay down alone.

39

THAT EVENING, SITTING in the garden, Mohammed said to Mr. David: I'm going to sleep in Benider tonight.

You never stay in one place any more, Mr. David told him. As soon as you come in you go out again. I never get a chance to talk to you. We never have any fun together. If I didn't love you I wouldn't have you here. But you've got to stay with me now and then.

I know, said Mohammed. It's my fault. You told me if I got married I'd be sorry. And you were right. But I didn't listen to you. I know, you give me money and food and clothes and the car, and I don't sleep with you every night. If you don't want me to stay on with you, just tell me.

No, Mohammed! Mr. David exclaimed. I never said that. You've always been good to me and my friends. That's not what I mean. I'd just like to see more of you.

Whatever you say, said Mohammed, standing up. You know what you want.

He went to the Zoco Chico and sat down in the Café Central. In a little while Hussein came by. Ahilán, Mohammed! Where have you been?

Spain.

Listen. I've got something to tell you. You're not going to like it, but don't blame me for it.

Blame you for what? said Mohammed. What is it?

Then Hussein said: I saw Mina with somebody. One day while you were away. I saw her talking with him. And she kissed him.

Never! Mohammed cried. It's not true!

I'm talking seriously, brother to brother. If you don't believe me, you can ask Chaib. He was with me.

It can't be, Mohammed kept saying.

I'm telling you I saw her with a man.

It wasn't Mina.

It was Mina. It was your wife talking to him. And afterwards she kissed him, and they separated. I saw it.

Not Mina.

Mohammed got up, paid the waiter and went to the house. Mina was there. He sat down and began to smoke a cigarette. He was sitting facing her, looking at her, thinking of Hussein's words. As he looked, his face became more fierce, until it seemed as if he might suddenly rise and kill her.

She stared at him. Why are you looking at me like that? What's the matter with you?

Nothing, he told her, turning his head away. I was thinking of something.

It's not true! she said. I saw you looking at me. You looked as if you hated me. I don't like your face. What's happened? Somebody's told you something.

When he heard these words, he said to himself: Hussein's not lying. It's true. He's right. She's been with somebody. In all the time I've known her she's never said such a thing, until now.

Can't you talk? Mina asked.

I'm thinking of something I forgot.

But what is it?

I tell you I wasn't looking at you, he said. I was just thinking, and my eyes got stuck on your eyes, and I stayed that way. And you thought I was looking at you. But I was thinking. I didn't even see you. I was somewhere else.

What was it you forgot? Money?

No. Some things I meant to buy in Spain at the last minute. Things I wanted. I was just thinking how I can't get them here.

What things?

A watch. A lady's watch with diamonds on it.

Allah! It must have been beautiful! she said.

I wanted to bring back two, he told her. One for you and one for your mother. Too bad. The next time I'll bring back two of them. Only who knows when that'll be?

Incha'Allah!

I'm going to sleep now, he said. I'm tired. I didn't sleep very well in Spain.

He put on his pyjamas and got into bed. Mina laid the baby in his crib. Then she got into bed, too. Mohammed kissed her, but her kisses were lifeless and chilly. He grew tired of kissing her, and drew back to look at her. She lay there as though she were thinking of something else. He felt his own heart growing cold, and the inside of his head seemed to come apart and be swimming around. How can this girl do this to me? he thought. I'm young and handsome and strong and clean.

He touched her again to be certain. Her flesh was cold. He got up from the bed and went out into the kitchen. In the closet on the shelf there were several bottles of red wine. He opened one and sat down at the table. He could hear it raining outside in the street. He cut himself some slices of cheese. He poured the wine into a tall glass and drank it off at one draught. Then he ate some cheese. Then he poured another glass of wine, and he went on doing it until both the cheese and the wine were gone. He went back into the other room and turned on the pale green light. He opened the window. The air that came in was cold and damp. He sat down in the chair facing Mina as she slept.

Later he went back to the kitchen and got another bottle of wine, and took it in with him to sit drinking it and watching Mina sleep.

Too bad, he said to his heart as he looked. What a world! In the beginning we were together. We lived another kind of life, with love in it. Whatever she wanted I gave her, and whatever I wanted she gave me. Clothes and money, words and love. And now if I put my lips on her lips, it's like kissing the cliffs at Merkala in January. If I lay my face against her face I get cold all over. There's no way of touching any part of her.

He had the glass of wine in his hand, and tears fell into it. He stared and went on staring at Mina, not moving his eyes from her face, until he saw fires lighted inside his head. He lifted the glass of wine and drank it. Then he set the glass on the table and began to drink from the bottle.

40

IN THE MORNING Mohammed was still sitting there with his head on the table. Mina got up.

Without waking him she washed and dressed, took the baby, and quietly went out.

At her mother's house she set the baby down on a mattress. Where's Mohammed? said her mother. Is he back?

I left him asleep in a chair, with his head on the table. Like a dog.

I pray to God the day will come soon when you'll be leaving him, her mother said.

Mother, I'm not going to leave him, Mina told her. The day I leave him, there'll be nothing left of him but his bones. I swear I'll kill him. She thought a moment. Or maybe I'll drive him crazy, so he'll go along the street talking to himself.

That's up to you, said her mother.

Early in the afternoon Mohammed woke up. He looked around for Mina, but she was not there. He dressed. Then he took a taxi out to Mstakhoche. Mina was still at her mother's house when he arrived.

Why didn't you wake me up? he asked her. You just went out and left me there.

Lalla Khaddouj told him: Mina said she didn't want to wake you up. She thought it was better to let you go on sleeping. She said you were tired.

That's true, Lalla, Mohammed said. Then to Mina he said: Let's go home. He took the baby in his arms, and they left.

At home they were sitting in the sala. Get me a cup of coffee, he told Mina.

I don't feel like it, Mina said.

He went to the kitchen and put the water on to boil. Then he came back and sat down. Mina, he said. We've been together for almost a year, so you can tell me the truth. Why can't you even look at me? What is it that's come between us?

You know what it is, she said. It's my mother. But that doesn't mean I'm going to let you go.

You're wrong, he told her. I can't go on hanging in the air like this forever. I try to kiss you, but I can't. I can't even touch you in bed. You don't want anything. You're dead. You weren't like this before. Don't you understand?

We're tired of it, that's all, she said.

It's not true! he cried. I'm not tired of it! And if two people are together, one of them can't just leave the other one by himself.

It's not that I don't love you, she said. I don't know what it is.

121

But your mother knows.

Get up! Get up! The water's all boiled away!

There was still water in the pot. He made two glasses of coffee and poured in some milk. After they had drunk the coffee he said: I'm going down to the hotel.

He kissed her hand, mocking her, and went out.

Mr. David was sitting at the bar, and Mohammed sat down with him.

I'm thinking of selling the hotel, he said, looking at Mohammed. And going to England.

Mohammed knew that he was saying this because he was annoyed with him.

I'm doing everything I can, he said. I'll be out of it soon.

But when? cried Mr. David. If only you could really finish with her!

Once I get rid of her I'll be all right.

Some people came into the bar then, and they did not go on talking. At two in the morning they shut the bar and went out to the bedroom in the garden. But Mr. David did not mention Mina at that time. The next day he and Mohammed drove to Souq el Had. They had a picnic lunch with them, and spent the day lying in the sun. Mohammed did not get back to the house in Benider until two o'clock the following morning.

41

MINA WAS SITTING in a chair. She looked pale. Didn't you sleep last night? Mohammed asked her.

No, she said. I wasn't sleepy. I've been sleeping a lot lately.

Mina, I'm going to take another trip with Mr. David. We're just going to Casablanca for a few days.

I see.

We're leaving tomorrow afternoon at six.

They went to bed. He tried to run his fingers over her body, but it gave him gooseflesh. He got up and went to lie in the sala on the couch. He did not even want to be in the same room with her.

They ate breakfast together, dressed the baby and themselves, and walked down to the beach called Las Palmeras. There they rented chairs and lay in the sun.

Now I know it's impossible for us to stay together, said Mohammed suddenly. But who's going to take the baby? I think I ought to have him. He'd have a better life with me. If you take him it'll be the end of him. You'll marry somebody who won't take care of him. And you can't help him. You're only a woman.

Mohammed, why are you talking about such things?

Because I can see them coming. The time is getting close. I've thought about it, and I know it's going to be soon.

Don't think I'm going to let you go, whatever you do.

We'll see, said Mohammed. Maybe we can still settle it. Who knows?

On the way home neither one of them spoke. When they were back at the house, he said to her: Why aren't you talking?

All you want to talk about is getting rid of me, and taking my baby away from me. The baby's mine. He's not yours.

Ah! Now you say he's not even mine?

He's not! she cried.

He turned away. Whenever you want to finish, just tell me, he said. I've got to go and help Mr. David get ready for the trip.

He filled a valise with clothes and carried it down to the hotel.

42

SOME TIME AFTER midnight that night Mohammed
went up to the house in Benider. He took out his key,
opened the door, and went in. It was dark inside.
Mina's mother lay asleep in the bed. The baby was in
his crib, but Mina was not there. He went out and
locked the door behind him, and started back to the
hotel. As he got to the bottom of the long staircase
that led down to the tannery, a taxi came up the ramp
from the waterfront and stopped. A girl got out. Mohammed backed into the shadows at the base of the
ramparts and watched. It was Mina. A man got out
after her and paid the taxi driver. Then the two stood
there in the street. They were saying good-bye, and
they had their arms around one another, kissing.
Finally the man walked back down the ramp, and
Mina began to climb the stairs.

Mohammed went on to the hotel. The door was
bolted. He rang the bell, and the night watchman
came.

What's the matter, Mohammed? I thought you
were sleeping at home tonight.

No. I'm going to sleep here.

The patron's gone to bed, said the watchman.

It doesn't matter, said Mohammed. He spent the night with Mr. David. The next afternoon he took his valise and went up to the house.

We didn't go anywhere, he said to Mina. Mr. David changed his mind. He had too much work to do. We'll probably go next week.

Mina's mother arrived while they were having lunch. Come in, said Mohammed. Sit down and have some lunch with us.

After Lalla Khaddouj had eaten, she said: Mina, can you come out to the house with me now?

Mina began getting ready to go out.

I've lost my key, Mohammed said to her. The key to the house here. Yesterday when I went out I must have put it into my pocket on top of my handkerchief.

While he was saying this he had his fingers around the key in his pocket.

Here's mine, said Mina. When you go out, lock the door.

Suppose you come back first and I'm not here? he said. You'd better take the key, because I might come back late.

All right. She took it back from him. Mina and her mother left. Shortly afterwards Mohammed went out for a walk in the Medina. After about a half hour he turned and walked back to the house. When he was inside, he picked up a small overnight bag that was lying on the floor in the bedroom, and opened the closet where Mina kept her gold bracelets and watches. He took them all out and put them into the plastic bag. Then he opened the box where his money was hidden, and put the money into the bag on top of the jewelry. He zipped the bag shut, pulled a few things off the shelves onto the floor and kicked them around, and went back out into the street. As he stepped through the doorway he hit the wood of the door jamb beside the lock and splintered it. He left the door slightly open and walked down the street.

At the hotel he hid the bag in a closet where Mr. David kept a great many things. He piled Mr. David's bags on top of it and left it there.

43

AT TWILIGHT MOHAMMED went up to the house in Benider.

Mohammed! Mina cried.

What's the matter?

Don't ask what's happened!

What is it?

When I got back I found the door broken open. I went straight to my gold, and it was gone. And your money, too. It's all gone.

Allah! What do you mean? It's impossible.

He ran in to look for his money, saw the empty box, and slapped his thigh. Who's been in here? he cried. You had nearly a million francs' worth of gold here! And I had two hundred thousand francs wrapped in paper in this box. I'm going now to the comisaría. They may be able to catch the thief before he sells anything.

Good, she said.

He went out, walked up to the Café de Paris, sat down and ordered a Flag Pils. He ordered a second bottle, watched the people going by, and went back to the house. On the way he looked in his wallet for a small piece of paper.

He found one, and held it in his hand as he went in.

What'd they say? Mina asked.

I went to the Brigada Criminal and told them everything. They wrote it all down and gave me this. He waved the paper and put it into his pocket. They'll find the man. Give them five or six days. They'll have him. They'll be telephoning to Casablanca or Rabat.

Mina went on thinking about it, and suddenly she began to cry.

There's no use in crying. Please. Don't make me even more unhappy. Every month I'll buy you something, and that way you'll collect a lot of new things.

She was listening.

Then if the police catch the man and you get back your own, you'll have more than ever.

For a moment Mina did not say anything. Then she said: The only person who could have taken that gold is you.

If I wanted to be as mean as you are, I'd say the same thing about your mother, Mohammed told her. I think she took it. Only let's not fight about it. I've had enough arguments with you. Let's try to be happy.

Mina was quiet for a moment. He turned to her and went on: So you thought I'd come and stolen your gold! Why would I have been giving you things all this time if I was going to come and take them away? You know I can get hold of more money than anybody in Tangier. I can charge tourists a thousand francs for a three-hundred-franc drink, and on top of that they'll tip me. Every day Mr. David gives me things to bring home. Food, money, clothes. I bring everything back here. Even if it's an apple, I don't eat it, do I? I bring it to you and watch you eat it. I don't even drink my glass of milk at breakfast time unless I know you have milk in the house. Sometimes at night when Señor David is asleep I get up and go out and sit in the garden. Everything is quiet, and I'm thinking of you. Something may happen to Mina. Somebody may hurt her, or she may get sick. And you! All you think is that I'm going to come and steal your jewelry. And when I was in Spain, you went to Emsallah, and you were standing in front of the Ciné Moghreb talking to a man. Yes or no?

No. It's a lie, she said. What time?

At ten at night.

By ten I was always in bed.

Last night when I said I was going to Casablanca, I came back here to the house at half past one and found your mother asleep in the bed, and the baby asleep in the crib, but I didn't find you.

Mina stared at him.

And then by the tannery I saw you getting out of a taxi. Yes, and he got out after you, and kissed you twice.

You're all wrong, Mohammed. That was my cousin. My father's brother's son. I went to their house. I've always gone to their house. He has four children now.

Yes. Your cousin.

Ask my mother. She'll tell you.

All right. We'll ask her.

Good.

Not now, said Mohammed. We'll go tomorrow. I thought I could trust you. I didn't believe you'd do that to me. Now why don't you get up and make some food so we can eat? Then I'll go to the hotel and you can sleep.

She got up and made him three fried eggs, and poured some tomato sauce over them. Then she got something for herself and sat down to eat with him. While he ate he talked.

I've spoiled you, he said. And that's why it's going to be hard for you when you leave me. And when you remember the words I'm saying now, you're going to be very sad.

Eat your food and stop talking, she told him. I never went out of the house while you were in Spain. And the man who brought me back in the taxi was my cousin. And he's got four children. And tomorrow my mother's going to be right here so you can ask her.

He finished his supper and went down to the hotel to spend the night with Mr. David. Before they went to bed Mr. David began again to talk about selling the hotel, and it took Mohammed a long time to make him stop.

44

EARLY IN THE morning Mohammed went back to the house in Benider. He tiptoed into the bedroom. Mina lay on her side, asleep. He went into the kitchen and made himself a glass of tea. Mina woke up and called to him to bring her some tea. They sat together having breakfast, and he glanced at her from time to time. She seemed nervous, and he imagined she was thinking: If I let him go, I'll lose him. Perhaps I should be good to him now, make him think I still love him. I'll bury my hatred in my heart for a while. I've got to make him think: She's happy again.

When Mina had finished her tea she got up and went over to him. Then she began to kiss him all over the face, so that the things he had just been imagining seemed to be completely true. He was pleased to think how right he had been, and how well he knew her. Knowing that he understood her game made him feel safe enough to pay attention to her kisses, and he began to feel happy. They went over to the bed, and in a moment they were both naked. She lay down and he bent over her, looking at her.

Mina, he was saying. The best body of all. The best girl. The only one I want, the only one I always want to see. He began to kiss her all over her body. Everywhere he could think of. Then he had his pleasure and was happy.

In the afternoon there was a knock at the door. Mohammed slipped on his trousers and went to open it. Mina's mother was standing there.

Ah, Lalla Khaddouj, said Mohammed.

She came in and he shut the door. Before she had sat down and before Mina could say anything, he started to speak.

I want to talk to you. I saw Mina with a man. And he told her everything he had seen.

Oh, that was her cousin, Lalla Khaddouj said straightway.

How's that? Her cousin! For a short moment he felt shame that he had been so harsh with Mina.

Mina burst out laughing, but Mohammed did not laugh. They've arranged this between them, he thought. I don't trust that old woman. They're both lying.

Lalla Khaddouj, you've got to have supper with us, he told her.

All right, Mohammed. But Si Ahmed's coming too in a little while.

So much the better, said Mohammed. He left Mina with her mother and went out to the market to buy the food. Soon he was back with chopped meat, new potatoes, grapes, raisins, onions and lettuce. He helped Mina prepare the food. Now and then she glanced at him with a question in her eyes, as if she were waiting to find out whether or not he believed her mother's story. When Si Ahmed came, Lalla Khaddouj went into the kitchen to help Mina, and Mohammed sat down in the sala with the old man.

How are you and Mina getting along? asked Si Ahmed.

Fifty per cent, said Mohammed. At least she does what she likes. If she doesn't have her way she gets sick. What can I do? Right now we're in the middle of a terrible mess.

Why? What's the matter?

Does your brother have a grown son?

My brother's boy? He's not so big. He's about twelve. The sisters are older.

I mean a married man with four children.

No, said Si Ahmed. Did they tell you that?

They didn't tell me anything. Only I saw a man yesterday who looked so much like your brother, I thought it must be his son. But he had four young ones.

No, no. My brother has no grown son.

Mina and her mother came in with the taifor. Si Ahmed broke the bread, and they all ate from the same dish. Presently Si Ahmed turned to Mina and said to her: Mina, why aren't you nicer to Mohammed? He's good to you. You always get your way.

He gives you whatever you want. You wouldn't find another boy who'd do all this for you. If you'd married anyone else, by this time you'd be having a terrible life, like everybody. You're living in heaven, let me tell you. He even lets you go out when you like and come in when you like.

All right, said Mina. And what am I doing to him? Why are you saying all this? What have I done that's so bad?

She hasn't done anything, said Mohammed. The poor girl's just unhappy.

Mina said nothing. They finished eating, drank a little tea, and then Si Ahmed said they must be going. They all got up. Bslemah. Bslemah. And Mina's mother and father went out.

45

LIFE WENT ON in the same way for Mohammed. Once in a while Mina would let him make love to her, but not very often. Sometimes he would spend a whole week at the hotel without going near the house in Benider. Then he would begin to wonder what she was doing, and he would go back and quarrel with her. After this he usually moved in for a few days. One evening when he was staying there in the house he said to her: Why don't we go to the cinema tonight? I feel like taking you out.

Good, she said. Only we'll have to go out to my mother's and leave Driss.

She got the baby ready, and Mohammed and she dressed carefully and went out. After they had taken the baby to Mstakhoche and left it there, Mina said: Let's not go to the cinema. Why don't we go somewhere we can sit and drink and dance if we feel like it?

Mohammed was happy to hear that she felt like drinking. Ouakha, he said. They walked to the hotel and went into the bar. Mr. David was there, and the barman, but there were no clients.

Oh, hello, said Mr. David when he saw Mina. Sit down and have a drink. Mohammed poured himself a whisky, and gave Mina some Cinzano. Mr. David put some records on the machine and turned down the lights. This made Mina want to dance. She asked Mr. David to dance with her. The trouble was that she did not know how. They stopped very soon, and had dinner. Then they went on drinking and laughing until three in the morning. A few Nazarenes came in.

I really need the car tonight, Mohammed told Mr. David. We have to go to Mstakhoche to get the baby, and Mina's drunk.

So I see, said Mr. David. Here are the keys.

Mohammed drove to Mstakhoche, parked the car, and went to knock on the door of Mina's father's house. Her mother got out of bed and handed him the baby, and he carried it back to the car where Mina was waiting.

They went home and put the baby in its crib.

Sit down, said Mina, when they were back in the sala. I want to talk to you.

Ouakha.

Mohammed, I don't like the way we're living.

I told you that first, a long time ago, he said.

I don't love you the way I did at the beginning.

I've told you that, too. Why don't you love me?

You did put a spell on me, Mohammed. You must have. I know you did. That's why it was so easy for my mother to pull us apart. If it had been real love, she couldn't have done anything.

Can't you forget that? he said.

I wish I could forget it. But it keeps coming into my head. You did put a spell on me.

No, Mina. It's Satan working inside you. That's why you go on thinking about these things. You have to try, at least. Try not to think about them.

I pray to Allah that He won't let you leave me. If you do, I'll never forget you.

If we're not together, it won't matter to me whether you're thinking of me or not, he told her. What difference will it make, if I don't even know where you are?

She did not answer.

Are you sleepy? he asked her.

Yes, she said.

Let's go to bed.

She got up and kissed him. They undressed and got into bed. They did everything they were used to doing, but it was not the way it had been. It was hard and cold, and when it was finished it was finished. There was nothing left. It was as if nothing had happened. For a long time Mohammed lay there, turning from side to side. Finally he put on the light and went into the kitchen for a glass of water. He went back to bed, and this time he fell asleep. It was about noon when they got up and dressed.

I've got to go and see my mother, said Mina.

The car was at the foot of the stairs. He drove her to Mstakhoche and then went to the hotel.

Good morning. I'm hungry, he said to Mr. David.

It's good afternoon now. Get yourself something in the kitchen.

Mohammed went out and made himself fried eggs, buttered toast and coffee. He carried it out to the bar and sat down with Mr. David.

Mohammed, I want to talk to you about that girl of yours. You know, she doesn't love you. I can tell you that. I was watching her last night, the way she acted with you. Europeans aren't all idiots, you know. Some of us can see what's going on.

I know Mina, Mohammed said. I can understand anybody. It's nothing new that she doesn't love me. I've known that for a long time. Ever since before the baby was born. Let's talk about something else.

I'm sorry. I'm not trying to upset you by talking about her. I'm warning you. She's no good for you. If you stay on with her, your life's just going to fall to pieces. You'll have nothing left in your bank account, and you know how you like to watch it grow.

Yes, said Mohammed. Long ago he had taken everything out of the bank.

You'll get rid of her, Mr. David said as if to comfort him. I know you'll find a way somehow.

46

MOHAMMED HAD WALKED out to Dradeb. Mustafa's house was on the side of the hill, in Derb Sidi Qacem. He pounded on the door. There were many small children playing and running up and down the steps of the street in front of the house. Mustafa opened the door.

Mohammed! How are you?

Fine.

What can I do for you? Come in.

I thought I'd come and see how you were, said Mohammed. He did not step inside.

I know why you came, Mustafa told him. Just tell me what you want me to do.

Mohammed hesitated. I want you to come with me. Out to Beni Makada. I want to see the witch. I want to talk to her.

Which one? I don't remember. The old hag?

Yes.

All right. Let's go now.

They went together and caught the bus. It was very

crowded and they did not stand near each other. In Beni Makada they walked to the house in the long street. Mustafa knocked on the door. The old woman opened it and motioned them in.

Do you remember me? Mohammed asked her.

Yes. You came once about a girl, and I did the work for you. And now what do you want?

I want you to do something to make me forget her. I don't want to think of her any more. I don't want to love her.

The old woman scratched her chin, and said: I don't know what to say. That kind of thing is very hard to do. I can try. You'd have to give me five thousand francs now. There are a lot of things to buy. If you want, I'll see what I can do with that much, and later we'll talk more about money.

How long will it take? said Mohammed.

Ten days, two weeks, a month. Who knows? If it works.

I can stand it that long, he said. He gave her five thousand francs. Bslemah.

Mohammed and Mustafa got back on the bus, rode into the city, and went to sit in a café.

Why do you want to get away from Mina? said Mustafa.

I can't leave her. I love her too much. But she's no good. If I don't do this I'll never get away from her. He told Mustafa what he had seen her do.

I can't believe Mina would do that, Mustafa said.

Have you finished your coffee? said Mohammed. Come around tomorrow or the next day.

Why don't I come now and have dinner? Mustafa said.

Good. I'll buy the food and be waiting for you.

When Mohammed got to the house Mina was not there. He took a kouffa and went to the market, where he bought lamb and olives. Back at the house he found that Mina had arrived. What's all that food? she said, looking into the kouffa.

I've got a friend coming for dinner.

She took the food into the kitchen and began to prepare it.

I'm going out for a minute, he said.

He ran and bought three bottles of expensive Spanish wine, carried them back and put them in the middle of the table. When Mina saw them she said: Very fine, indeed! And what does this mean?

Once a year it doesn't hurt.

It's all we needed.

You've got nothing to do with it, he told her. This is for us. If you want to eat with us, good. If you don't you can eat in the other room or go to bed.

I see, she said.

There was a knock at the door. Come in! Sit down!

Mustafa came in. This is my wife, said Mohammed. Mustafa is an old friend of mine.

Mustafa took her hand.

They sat down and talked until Mina brought in the food. Mohammed opened one of the bottles and began to pour wine into the glasses. Soon the room was full of laughter.

What are you laughing about? demanded Mina. You've only had one glass each, and you're already drunk?

No, said Mohammed. It's not the wine. What we're laughing at is something we remembered. One time when we were drinking together we saw somebody who made us laugh.

And I'm the person, said Mina, looking at him.

No, Mina! Mustafa cried. We were talking about something else. How can you think that? We were remembering something that happened a long time ago. There was a Spaniard who used to dance in a bar, and whenever he began to dance he would go: Eheh! Eheh! Eheh! and we would always laugh.

I'm sorry, said Mina. And she began to talk and joke with them. They finished the first bottle and the second, and they began on the third.

Why don't we go out for a while and drink somewhere else? said Mustafa.

It depends on Mina, said Mohammed. Ask her.

He's not going out now, she said. He's going to bed.

Mustafa said good night to them and went out. Mohammed bolted the door.

You don't see anything wrong with that? said Mina.

Bringing your friends off the street into the house? Getting drunk in the house where your son is sleeping? You could use the money for a lot of better things. And your friend was drinking in front of me.

What do you mean? You were drinking too, weren't you?

Mina did not answer. A minute later she said: If you try to divorce me I'll say no. You're going to pay money.

I see, said Mohammed.

47

THE NEXT AFTERNOON Mohammed went to the courtyard of the notaries.

What do you want?

I've been living with a girl now for a year, he said, and I'm going to leave her.

Have you got your marriage certificate with you? The one the qadi gave you?

No, said Mohammed. I never went to get it.

Then the marriage is not official, said the notary. You're only living with the girl. Have you any children?

One.

Why do you want to leave her? Why don't you legalize the marriage?

She's got somebody else.

Wait, said the notary. I'll have to send for the girl.

About an hour later the chaouch came back with Mina. She had the baby in her arms and looked very angry.

The notary told her: This man wants to finish with you.

I won't leave, she cried. I have a baby, and the baby's got to have a father. Even without the baby, I wouldn't leave him.

The notary watched Mina closely. You're being very foolish, the notary said. He's willing to give you everything in the house.

Mina did not reply. The notary turned to Mohammed and shrugged his shoulders. You'll have to try and put up with her. Perhaps you should be kinder to her. You'll come to some sort of understanding between you. You should try to get along together, because now you have a child, and you'll have more. And you should go to the qadi and get your marriage paper.

Mohammed could see it was of no use. Yes, Sidi, he said.

Come on, he told Mina.

When they were back in the house, Mina looked at him and said: Here I am. Where did that get you? Nowhere.

No. Nowhere, said Mohammed. You won. You were always lucky, weren't you?

48

IT WAS EIGHT o'clock, and Mina was not yet at the house in Benider. Even though he knew she was not there, Mohammed looked behind the doors and in each place where she might be hidden. He went out into the street and took a taxi to Mstakhoche. At Mina's house he knocked. Her mother opened the door.

Is Mina here?

No.

He went into town on foot. When he got to the middle of the Boulevard Pasteur, he saw Mina coming towards him, carrying the baby in her arms. She was dressed in a djellaba and her face was covered. This surprised him, for she wore Moslem clothing only at festivals.

Where have you been? he asked her.

Taking a walk.

What kind of hour is this to be taking a walk? It's been dark for a long time.

I didn't think you'd be back, she said. I went out for a walk.

Let's go, he told her.

When they got home, she took off her djellaba and veil, and put the baby to bed.

Tell me where you've been, said Mohammed.

For a walk.

Where did you go and who were you with?

He took off his jacket.

Is it any of your business? she said. I was taking a walk with someone.

He slapped her so hard that the blood began to run out of her nostrils. She burst out crying, and he began to feel sorry for her. He took out his handkerchief and tried to stop the blood. Then he wiped her face. He hugged her tightly. Forgive me, he said. I'm sorry.

He kissed her.

It's all right, she said. Now get away from me.

She went into the kitchen and put cold water on her face. He followed her.

Tell me the truth, Mina. Where were you?

All right, I'll tell you. I went to see a Spanish woman who lives opposite the Ciné Goya. She's a seamstress. I wanted to see her about making me a suit. But I stayed too long.

How much did she want? Does she buy the material?

No. I saw what I want on the Boulevard. It's seven thousand francs a meter. I need three meters, and she wants eight thousand to make it. But she does very good work.

I may be able to get it from the Nazarene, said Mohammed.

Whenever you have the money, she said. There's no hurry.

They went to bed. Suddenly Mina seized Mohammed and began to kiss him very hard, saying many sweet words. But when he tried to take her she slipped away. Immediately he felt a pain like fire in his heart. Soon she was asleep. He could only lie there. And he got up and turned on the light and sat down in a chair beside the bed. He looked at her. She was perfect.

He stayed a long time watching Mina sleep. Then he got up, leaned over and kissed her forehead, saying aloud: Too bad.

He meant: Too bad your mother has ruined everything. He turned out the light, and went into the kitchen, shutting the door behind him. There was a bottle of Coñac Fundador on the shelf. He took it and sat down. And he began to drink, so that he could forget everything. As soon as he crushed out one cigarette he lit another. In an hour he had smoked a pack. He thought of the unhappy life he was living, and it seemed to him that his life would be the way he wanted it only when he got rid of Mina and the baby. He remembered his dream. The figure in white had told him he was about to begin a new life. He wondered if the witch's magic had begun to take effect. I've got to get free, he told himself.

He emptied the last drops of cognac into his glass, drank them, and got up. He opened the kitchen door and went into the bedroom, drunk. He turned on the light again and looked down at Mina. Then he tiptoed over to the crib and looked a long time at Driss. How am I going to leave him? he thought. I'll stay until I catch her talking to someone again, and then I'll kill her.

He left the crib and went back to the bed. As he looked at Mina he thought of how pleasant it would be to strangle her. But he was afraid, and could not move. The fear made him think again: If I hold out I can win. If a man can keep going long enough he can win. She'll get no money from me.

He went back to the kitchen and slept sitting in the chair with his head on the table. At ten in the morning Mina got up. She found him there asleep.

Mohammed, Mohammed, she said, trying to wake him up.

What?

Why don't you lie in the bed?

He went and got into the bed. She began to wash the dishes. Then she sat down in a chair beside the bed, while Mohammed slept and the baby lay on the rug. She was embroidering a piece of cloth.

Finally Mohammed opened his eyes. Have you been sitting here long? he asked her.

I'm making something. She showed him the handkerchief she was embroidering. I'm finishing it, she told him.

He got up and washed. After lunch he said: Shall we go out? Do you want to take a walk?

Tomorrow.

I'll see you later, he told her.

49

MR. DAVID WAS in the bar. When he saw Mohammed come in he called to him. Listen, he said. Some friends of mine from England have come. I used to go to school with them. They want me to take them down to Marrakesh and maybe to the Sahara. Can you take charge of the hotel while I'm away? You'll have to keep your eyes open. I don't want any fights or noise. Everything's got to go on the way it always does. The bar's the hardest part.

Don't even think about it. I'll take care of everything, said Mohammed.

I know. You're careful.

After he shut the bar that night, Mr. David gave Mohammed the cash box and the accounts. I've got no idea how long I'll be gone, he told him. It may be two weeks or it may be two days. It depends on how it all turns out. Whenever they want to come back they'll come back.

He and Mohammed went in to sleep. When Mohammed awoke the bed was empty. He sat around the hotel all day, drinking. When evening came he went into the bar and washed all the glasses and shined up the bottles. Around nine o'clock a few people came in, but they did not stay very long. He felt sleepy and he closed the bar early. Then instead of going home he went in and slept in Mr. David's bed.

At one the next afternoon Mina arrived with the baby. Mohammed was having his breakfast. Hello, Mina, he said. What's the matter?

Why didn't you come home last night? she demanded.

I was too tired. I slept here.

You brought some girl in. The Christian isn't here now.

You haven't got the right to say that! You know I've got no girls.

You're lying.

That's all right, he said. You can think whatever you want to think, señora.

Aren't you ever coming home? she said.

I'm coming now if you'll wait a minute. He counted the money in the cash box and handed the box to Abdelkrim the barman. Let's go, he said.

Take the baby, Mina told him. He took the baby and carried him in his arms through the streets.

That evening, sitting in the house at Benider, Mina said: This time I'll forgive you. But the next time you sleep away from the house you'll see. Unless the Christian is there too.

Listen, he said. I'm not your slave. I'm free. I can

sleep here or where I like. It's all the same anyway. There was nobody in the hotel, and there's nobody here. If you had a heart that was still alive, even though you don't love me you could at least do me a favor in bed, and move a little when I'm with you, instead of pretending you're not there. Any other man would have left you the first time you did that to him. Even animals know how to make love.

As he talked his voice grew more bitter.

My cousin, he mimicked. My father's brother's son. I swear he has four children. What sort of girl would do a thing like that? With a piece of garbage! He may have syphilis or yaws. Maybe he doesn't wash himself. And you go to bed with him and then come into your husband's house. Your handsome husband that you'll never leave! He laughed. But your handsome husband knows what women are like. You're treacherous, and I'm too tired to go on trying to watch you. There are plenty of girls waiting. Half a word and I'm married. I wanted to have a real marriage with papers, so we could have some sort of life and live in the real world. But you saw everything backwards. You did everything without thinking first. That's why you'll always lose.

She looked at him. You understand, she began.

What?

If you run away from me I'll find you and kill you. You understand?

I'll die the way I'm meant to die, he said. Not until

then. You don't exist. I'm going to leave you. He pounded his palm with his fist. And forget you. And never see your face or hear your voice again. You won't know the difference. When I come in, you look as if you'd never seen me before. Who's that? Just somebody who comes in and goes out. Just a shadow. When he comes and wants a clean shirt there aren't any clean shirts, and when he wants his trousers pressed they stay wrinkled. All my clothes are dirty! Everything! If I didn't pack them up myself and take them down to the hotel with me and give them to the black woman they'd always be dirty. I've had enough of it.

He stood up.

Is that all? she said.

That's all.

50

MOHAMMED WENT DOWN to the hotel. It was a cold rainy night, and practically no one came into the bar. Soon he shut it and went in to bed. The next morning early he got up and went to the courtyard of the notaries.

The notary looked up. What is it? he said frowning.

I'd like to speak with you, but alone, said Mohammed.

Ouakha. He took Mohammed into another room. It was small and empty.

I'm leaving that girl, said Mohammed. I can't live with her any longer. She's going with other men. I can't stay with a girl like that.

You told me the whole story, said the notary. And you've got to try to make things better between you.

Mohammed took out his wallet and handed a ten thousand franc note to him. This is your propina, he said. And I'd like to know how much I've got to pay her.

Let me see. There would be one month at fifteen

thousand. And four months for the baby would be twenty thousand. That's thirty-five thousand.

I'll give her forty to get out right away. She can take anything in the house she wants. She can have it all.

The notary sent for Mina's father while Mohammed waited in his office. Two or three hours afterwards the old man came in. The notary told him that the marriage had been canceled, and he said: Yes. It's all right.

Then Mohammed and Si Ahmed went together to the house in Benider, and Si Ahmed told Mina what had happened. She jumped up and quickly began to gather together all the best things in the house.

Mohammed was watching her. Why don't you take the other things, too? he said. Take everything.

He went out and got a large taxi. Then he came back to the house and helped Mina pack the things she wanted. When all the suitcases and boxes and baskets were full he carried them down to the waterfront where the taxi was waiting. He had to make four round trips. Mina and her father sat in the taxi.

I'm sorry, Mohammed told Si Ahmed. He kissed the baby, and the taxi drove away.

He went back to the house and packed his clothes into his valises, and carried it all in a taxi to the hotel. Then he went up to the Joteya and spoke with an auctioneer. He took the man back with him to Benider and showed him the furniture.

I'll buy it, said the auctioneer. He looked at the

radio and the phonograph and the tables and chairs and rugs. I'll give you a hundred thousand.

If that's all you can pay, let's forget it, said Mohammed. I can sell the things.

What's your last price? the man asked him. Go on. Tell me.

A hundred and forty thousand buys it all.

No! the man said. Then he turned and said: All right. I'll take it. He pulled out a hundred and forty thousand francs and gave them to him. Mohammed tucked the bills into his wallet. The auctioneer went and got some men, and they carried everything out of the house. Then Mohammed locked the door from the outside. He went to Dradeb and said to Mustafa: Take your keys. I'm not going back there. Mustafa tried to find out from him what had happened, but he waved and walked away.

51

THAT NIGHT AFTER Mohammed had opened the
bar, two Americans came in and sat down. What will
you have? he asked them.

Whisky with soda and ice, they said. What will you
drink?

Thank you. I'll take whisky, too. He drank it, and
then offered them another whisky. They invited him,
he invited them, back and forth. They went on drinking until it was very late. When the Americans had
gone and he was alone in the bar, he sat down and
poured himself a large glass of straight whisky. As he
drank it he listened to the clock ticking behind the
bar. He still had not heard from Mr. David. He got up
and put on a record. It was Farid el Atrache singing
"Hekayats Gharrami." He listened to the words and
grew sad. The music filled the room. He had the glass
in his hand, and his head was spinning. And in a little
while he found his hand gripping the glass with such
force that it broke. He went into Mr. David's room
and fell onto the bed. The blood was coming out of
his hand. At two o'clock the next afternoon he opened

his eyes and saw the sheets covered with blood. His hand ached. It was cut in three places. He took a taxi out to the Spanish Hospital and had them clean and bandage his hand. When he got back to the hotel he washed the sheets and hung them in the garden to dry.

During the early part of the evening Mohammed sat in the bar alone, waiting for customers to come in. Instead, two Moslem boys whom he knew slightly arrived, sat down at the bar and began to talk with him.

We're having a little party Saturday night, they told him. And you've got to come.

Neither Brahim nor Mokhtar had ever invited him before, and he thought it was strange that they should invite him now.

I won't be able to stay very late, that's all, he said. I have to be back here to take care of the hotel. The only thing the night watchman knows how to do is turn off the light over the front door. I have to do everything else myself.

That's all right, they said. Just be sure and come.

He poured three whiskies, one for each of them and one for him. Two Frenchmen came in. Mohammed served them. Brahim stood up saying: I've got something to do, and went out. Mokhtar stayed behind. Soon he leaned across the bar towards Mohammed. Listen, he said. There's a girl out looking for you to kill you. She's sworn to do it. She's got three or four other girls working for her, all whores, but you don't know any of them. Each one has the tsoukil ready to give you. Wherever they find you, they'll wait till you're drunk. Once it's inside you you're dead, so be careful.

Thanks for telling me, said Mohammed. He looked at Mokhtar suspiciously, wondering why he had stayed behind to tell him this.

I heard the story. I wanted to tell you because you're a friend of mine, said Mokhtar. Be very careful.

I will.

Allah ihennik.

Bslemah.

52

SEVERAL DAYS PASSED. On Saturday afternoon while Mohammed was having his breakfast he looked up. Mr. David was standing in front of him.

How are you, Mohammed? He sat down beside him. How did everything go?

Everything went well. Nothing happened. Everybody's happy.

That's what I wanted to hear! said Mr. David, patting his shoulder.

But you don't know why I'm happy.

No. Why?

You can't guess?

The girl's gone?

I'm free!

Mr. David hugged him. I can't believe it, he said, shaking his head.

I told you I'd get rid of her, said Mohammed, laughing. He went to the bar, and a moment later he called to Mr. David: Here are the accounts. Mr. David said they could wait until later, but Mohammed insisted, and so he went and examined them then, and found everything in order. He counted the money and turned to Mohammed.

Mil gracias, Mohammed. Everything is perfect. You always do everything right. He took out thirty thousand francs and handed them to Mohammed. A little present for you, he said.

Shortly afterwards Mohammed went out. As he was walking through the Zoco de Fuera he heard someone call his name. It was Mokhtar, and Brahim was with him. He stopped to talk with them.

Don't forget to come to Dradeb tonight, they said.

A girl came up and greeted them. Where's the party tonight? she asked them.

We're having it at the house in Dradeb, they told her.

I'll be there, she said.

Mohammed was looking at her. I'm going to spend the night with this one, he thought. What's your name? he asked her.

Melika.

You've got to sit beside me tonight, he said. I'm asking you now. Don't sit with anybody else.

She smiled. Ouakha.

Would you like to take a walk? he asked her.

All right.

They said good-bye to Mohktar and Brahim and started up the street. My name is Mohammed, he said.

Yes.

Don't you have any other clothes? He was looking at her old European sweater and skirt. Those things aren't right for you.

Yes, of course, she said. I have other things.

I'll go with you and wait while you change, and then we'll go somewhere good.

He waited in a street of Emsallah while she disappeared down an alley to her house and changed her clothes. Finally she came back, looking much better, except that she was still wearing the same worn and dirty shoes.

Are those the only shoes you've got? he said.

Yes.

Haven't you got a handbag?

No.

Come on, he said. He had hidden the money he had got for the furniture with the gold and the two hundred thousand francs in Mr. David's closet, but in his pocket he had what Mr. David had just given him. They went into the Bata store opposite the Hotel Minzah, and she bought a pair of shoes. Then they went to an Italian in the Boulevard Mohammed Khamiss and got a handbag and a big square silk handkerchief. Melika was delighted.

Now come with me, he said. He took her into the Café de Paris and sat down. But the place was crowded with Europeans, and Mohammed did not feel like talking. They drank their coffee and ate their pastries quickly.

Let's go up to Sidi Amar, he told her.

All right.

They got into a taxi and drove up to the top of the mountain, where there was a bar that belonged to a Negro from America. He was a friend of Mohammed's. They sat in a booth and ordered drinks. Then the American saw Mohammed and called to him. Mohammed left his drink on the table and went over to the bar. Now and then he looked into the mirror behind the bar and watched Melika sitting alone at the table. If she had something to put into his drink, this was the time when she would do it. But she merely sat there. After a while he went back to the table. They had another drink and joked a while, and then Mohammed telephoned for a taxi.

53

THEY DROVE DOWN to a house in the Calle Canarias at Dradeb. A great many young men and girls were inside drinking. There was a bar with bottles of wine set out. A row of braziers lined one end of the room, and the steam came up from the pots of food cooking on the coals.

Mohammed and Melika went around greeting people, and then they sat down side by side on the cushions. Everyone drank and everyone ate, and there was dancing and laughter. At two o'clock Mohammed got up. I've got to go, he said.

Melika and Mohammed said good-bye to their friends. When they were in the street, he said to her: I'll take you home.

After a time they found a taxi and went to Emsallah. They got out and walked through the alleys. The moon was very bright and the shadows very dark.

Take me to the door, she said.

They went into a long narrow alley, and she stopped in front of a door and took out her keys. She opened it, stepped inside, and said: Come in.

He found himself in a comfortable room with a thick rug on the floor. Through an archway he could see a huge bed with gauze curtains around it and a light inside. There was a sewing machine by the bed. The walls were covered with big framed photographs, and there were two long mirrors.

This is a fine place, said Mohammed.

Come in here, she said, and she led him into her bedroom. There he sat in a chair and smoked a cigarette while she undressed. She took off everything but her pink underpants. And as she did this she kept her eyes on his face.

He looked back at her. She came over to him and sat down in his lap. He put his arms around her, but did not move.

He could not do anything with her, he told himself. The same thing would happen again. He would find himself loving her and then lose her to someone else. But I've got to do it, he thought. If I don't, she'll say I'm not a man. He took her head between his hands and stroked her hair. Then he kissed her. She bit his lips. He cried out and she laughed. He got up and undressed, leaving on only his shorts. She stared at him and ran her hands over his chest. You've got a beautiful body, she told him. I love it! Muscles everywhere.

Let's talk about your body, he said.

She pulled back the curtain around the bed, and they climbed in. Then she shut the curtain. He helped her take off her underpants. As soon as she lay back naked, he seized her and pulled her on to him. She kissed him and played such serious games with him that his thoughts went back to Mina, and it seemed to him that Melika was like Mina, that she was doing everything the way Mina had done it. He climbed on top of her and pushed into her flesh, imagining that she was really Mina. When he was finished they lay together, kissing, and each kiss lasted a long time. At the end he went to sleep still lying on her flesh.

He was asleep, and Melika was saying: Mohammed, Mohammed.

I want to sleep, he murmured. Then he raised his head. What's the matter?

Nothing. Are you angry?

What do you mean? I'm happy! How could I be angry with you? I've got something new in my life now. I feel as if something might happen at last.

I'm going to tell you the truth, she said. Listen to me.

What?

Mina gave me tsoukil to give you. Here it is.

She picked up a small cloth bundle that lay on the night table, laid it on the pillow, and unwrapped it. He stared at the powder inside.

I couldn't make myself do it, she said. I was going to put it in your drink in the bar up at Sidi Amar, but it just stayed in my hand. She folded the cloth again and laid it on the table.

Mina has a lot of friends, she went on. She called us all in to hear her make a vow. And she swore in front of us that she was going to kill you, and made us promise to help her. Her girls all know you by sight. You've got to look out for yourself.

Mohammed kissed her cheek. There's no way to repay such a favor! he said. You're a wonderful girl!

The important thing is that you've got to watch everybody every minute, she told him.

He put his arms around her and kissed her again, and they went to sleep. In the morning they awoke and began to kiss again. When they had finished doing everything, Mohammed got up and washed. Then he put on his clothes.

Are you going? she said.

Yes.

When can I see you?

I can come by tonight. But not early. I might come at three. Or it might be two or four. I don't know.

Here's the key, she said.

You live here alone?

Yes. I live alone.

Haven't you got anybody? A boy friend, or a husband?

Look. I'm not going to pretend with you. I work in the street. If I give you the key it's because I want you to have it. I want you to be with me. But you'll do as you like.

He put his hand into his pocket and brought out

five thousand francs. Here, he said. Buy some food. I'll be back later.

Ouakha. Incha'Allah.

He went down to the hotel and had lunch with Mr. David. Why don't we take a drive? Mr. David asked him.

All right.

He handed Mohammed the car keys. You drive, he said.

They went out into the country and took the airport road to El Achaqal. There they sat in the bar on top of the cliff and ordered two cognacs. They looked out at the sea. The wind that blew in through the windows smelled good.

Think of it, Mohammed! said Mr. David. We've been together more than five years! And you still mean more to me than anybody in my family.

You mean a lot to me too, Mohammed told him. You're something very important in my life. Not even my father has ever done so much for me. I have everything I want, go where I like, do as I please. How could anybody not love a man who gave him all that?

Yes, I suppose that's true, said Mr. David. They drank their cognacs and had others, and began to feel very well. When they left the café, they went out with their arms around each other, singing. As Mohammed drove he went on with the song. They sped around the curves near Cape Spartel on two wheels. At the hotel they surprised people walking past by going in together singing. They opened the bar and had some more cognac. The customers began to arrive. It was a noisy night, but by half past two everyone had left. They shut the bar. Then Mohammed said: Excuse me. I've got to go somewhere.

What, again? said Mr. David.

Yes, Mohammed said. Goodnight.

54

MOHAMMED WALKED TO the alley in Emsallah, unlocked the door, and went in. Melika was sitting on
the couch.

Haven't you gone to bed yet? said Mohammed.

I was waiting for you to come. Do you want some
supper?

No. I'm not hungry. I'm just sleepy. He hoped she
would not see that he was drunk.

They got into bed. This time he lay face upward,
and she was stretched out on top of him. They kissed
a while, and then he rolled her over and made her
happy. Then they slept.

The next afternoon at one o'clock they got up.
Mohammed gave her a little money and said he would
be back later.

When he went into the hotel Mr. David told him
that a Moslem woman had come that morning and
given him a letter she said was for Mohammed.

Where is it?

He opened it. It was a very polite letter written in
Arabic. It said that the friends who had invited him to

their mahal in Dradeb the night before last would like him to come again tonight, and that they hoped he would not disappoint them. They counted on his coming.

I won't be here tonight, he told Mr. David. I've got to go somewhere.

I see. Tell Abdallah he'll have to stay.

At seven in the evening he took the car and drove out to Dradeb. He knocked and was let in. Again there were many people in the mahal. A few of them were friends of his, but most of them he did not know. He took a glass of wine, and looked at the girl who was pouring it. When Moslem boys and girls get drunk together, it is not polite for anyone to have his own glass. Everyone must drink out of the same glass. First one drinks, and then another, in turn. One glass for everybody, and only one girl pouring the wine. It is done this way so there is less chance of being poisoned. Still Mohammed watched the girl who was pouring. And she must have taken a bottle that had only a little wine left in it, and dropped the powder into the bottle, and then left the bottle nearby with the other empty bottles. By this time Mohammed had stopped watching her. He was singing with his friends. And the next time it was his turn to drink from the glass, he let her fill it without paying attention. And she must have filled it from the bottle that had only a little wine in it. He was hot. He reached out for the glass and took it from her hand. He drank it and gave her back the glass.

It was about two o'clock in the morning. I've got to leave, he said.

When he had thanked Brahim and Mokhtar and said good-bye, he went out and got into the car. He drove as far into Emsallah as he could, parked the car, and walked along the alleys. He was cold. By the time he got to the house he was colder, so cold that he could not get the key out of his pocket. He pounded on the door.

Melika was inside. Who is it? she said.

Me.

She opened the door. Ah! she cried. What's the matter with you?

I'm sick, he said. I've never felt so cold.

She helped him undress and got him into bed. Cover me up, he kept saying, and she piled many blankets on top of him.

She was sitting beside him, saying: What's the matter with you? What is it? And he was falling asleep in the cold. And as he slept he groaned.

The next morning about nine o'clock, in spite of all Melika said, he got up and went out to a café that was nearby in the quarter. He went inside and sat in a chair. Suddenly he began to vomit. When he looked down, he saw that what he had vomited was blood. Blood was running from his nose. He fell forward onto the floor.

An ambulance finally arrived, and they took him to the Kortobi Hospital.

174

55

JUST AFTER THE ambulance had left, Melika went out of her house to go to the market. When she got to the café she saw the crowd of people, and then she looked inside and saw all the blood.

Who was it? she said. Poor thing!

A boy who knew that Mohammed was living with her came over and told her what had happened.

What? she cried.

She got into a taxi and went to the hospital. Mohammed was in a very bad state. We don't know now, they told her.

She kept looking at Mohmmaed. He can't talk, she thought. That's it. Mina's managed to do it.

She took another taxi down to Emsallah to see a Djibli who sold charcoal in a side street.

What can you give somebody's who's taken tsoukil? she said. How can you save him?

I have a very old oil, he said. And some fifty-year-old sminn.

In the hospital the doctors pumped Mohammed's stomach and did many things to him. After a few hours he woke up. I want to go home, he told them.

A little later Melika arrived in her taxi, and they let him go out with her. She took him home to her house and put him into bed. Then she went out and got the Djibli charcoal seller and brought him back to the house with her.

The Djibli sat down beside the bed and took out his oil. Mohammed drank it and ate the sminn. The Djibli sat waiting. Soon Mohammed got up and went into the bathroom. He began to vomit, and he went on vomiting. When he came out they made him eat. Then he vomited again. He ate, rose, vomited, came back and ate again, rose and vomited, several times. Then the Djibli said: Now drink a large glass of cold water. Mohammed drank the water and lay down.

We'll leave him like that, said the Djibli.

In the morning when Mohammed woke up, he had no more pain, and he felt warm and alive. Melika saw that he was awake and looked at him closely. How are you? she asked him.

I feel fine now, only I'm a little dizzy, he said. A lot better than yesterday! I had a bad time.

I told you to be careful! I was so worried!

He hugged her and kissed her. Let's go out for a walk, he said.

Not today. You're not well enough.

I've got to go to the hotel anyway, he said. I'll only stay a little while, and then I'll be back.

When Mr. David saw Mohammed, he began

straightway to ask him questions. Where have you been? What's the matter with you? You're so pale!

Mohammed sat down and told him the story. Sometimes he seemed to forget it. He would stop and repeat the last sentence before going on. When he had finished, Mr. David said: It was Mina who did that?

Yes.

I told you to look out for that little bitch. She's no good. From now on you've got to be careful every minute. You're to young to die or have your health ruined. You think you're a man, but you're not. You're just a boy. You're lucky not to be dead.

It was a girl. She saved my life. She did everything for me.

Who's this one?

Mina gave her the tsoukil to give me. But at the last minute she was afraid and didn't do it. So she told me about it, and showed it to me.

She sounds very dangerous to me, said Mr. David. Don't trust her. Don't trust any woman. Why don't you save your money? One girl after another, and no rest in between. How do you expect to stay strong and healthy? Sitting up all night in filthy rooms drinking. Take care of yourself. You'll never be anything this way.

Mohammed sighed. I know, he said.

After a time, he said he was tired. I'm going back to Emsallah and go to bed, he told Mr. David.

56

MOHAMMED WAS LIVING with Melika, but he was not happy. He kept telling himself that he did not want to fall in love with her. He would walk along the street talking out loud to himself, saying: I don't want any more trouble. I'll never fall in love again with any girl or woman. Never. Here's a girl who makes her living in the street. She saw I was with an Englishman who gives me everything. She sees that I give her money. She knows how I spoiled Mina when she was with me. And she wants me to fall in love with her so she can be another Mina. And before it's over she'll have me on the end of a string. I've got to finish with her! I've got to finish it!

He began to plan ways of getting rid of Melika. The more he thought about it, the more eager he was to get it over with. It seemed to him that once he had freed himself from her he could begin once more to live.

One night when Mohammed was being barman, serving drinks to the Nazarenes, Mr. David came into the bar and stood watching him for a while. Then he went behind the bar and spoke with him.

Mohammed, he said. I don't like the way things are going.

Why? What have I done? said Mohammed.

You're acting crazy. I don't know what's wrong with you. When you get drunk your language is terrible. I don't want to hear such things in the bar.

If you don't want me to drink here, I won't, said Mohammed.

I think it would be better if you didn't.

That's all right.

After this whenever a Nazarene invited Mohammed to have a drink with him at the bar, he said: I'm sorry. It's forbidden. During the weeks that followed many Nazarenes offered him drinks, and he always gave the same reply. When they heard this, some of them were indignant and spoke to Mr. David about it. It's a shame, they would say. He's so amusing when he's had a few drinks. And the women would cry: Oh, let the poor boy have a drink! Some of them said the bar was not the same now that Mohammed always had such a sad face.

One night a group of drunken Englishmen announced that if Mohammed were not given a drink right away, they would go to another bar down the street where there was a barman who was able to smile.

But Mohammed's impossible when he drinks! Mr. David cried. He gets insolent and starts fights. You don't have to put up with him afterwards, but I do.

Then he shrugged and went over to the bar. You can have a drink if you want, he told Mohammed. I don't mind.

That's all right, said Mohammed. He poured himself a straight whisky and drank it. The Englishmen stayed on at the bar and everyone was happy.

After they had closed for the night, Mr. David went out to the Bar Parade to keep an appointment. Mohammed stayed behind and drank some more. Then he decided to go out. He shut the front door behind him and walked down to the Avenida de España. The wind was making a great noise in the palm trees there.

He found a taxi and told the driver to go to Emsallah.

He got out and went into the alleys. As he walked along he began to say to himself: No, I won't go in. I don't want to see her. I'm afraid of her.

Before he got to the house he turned around and walked the other way.

57

ONE MORNING NOT long afterwards while Mohammed was having his breakfast in the bar he heard the bell ring. He went out and found Melika in the doorway.

There was no one else around at that moment, and so he said: Come in. He led her into the bar and she sat down with him. He gave her a glass of coffee and went on with his breakfast.

How are you? he asked her.

It's so long since I've seen you, she said. I was afraid something had happened to you, or that you were sick again.

I'm all right. Only it's the tourist season and the hotel is full of Nazarenes every night, and I've been too busy to go anywhere.

You could always have taken a taxi to Emsallah and kept it waiting, and come to see me just for a minute. So I'd have known you were alive, at least. I've been waiting and waiting. She kept looking at him. Are you sure you're all right?

He knew she was talking about the tsoukil, which can leave a man with many things wrong. And he knew that since he had come out of the hospital he had often been dizzy and found himself talking aloud when there was no one there to hear him. He lighted a cigarette.

A taxi to Emsallah? he said. I didn't think of it. Why don't we go out?

They took a long walk, along the beach to the Monopolio and then up to the Boulevard Pasteur. When they came to the park above the harbor they sat down on a bench there and looked out at the water.

You don't seem happy, Mohammed, she said at last.

Melika, I've got something to say to you, and you're going to be upset.

No, no, Mohammed. Tell me.

This is something very serious. I can't see you any more. I keep thinking of Mina. You've been good to me and I love you. But we can't see each other. If you meet me in the street, a glance is enough. If you ever need anything, come and tell me, and I'll always be ready to help if I can. I hope you understand.

She had begun to cry. He touched her arm. It's all right, she said. It's nothing.

They got up. She was still crying.

Don't cry, he said. He wanted to go quickly. Allah ihennik.

He walked away. She sat down again on the bench.

When he got up onto the pavement under the trees he stood still a moment and looked back. It made him ill to see her sitting there alone with her hand over her eyes, but he walked on.

58

MOHAMMED SAT IN the bar at the hotel, regretting what he had just done. I could have lived with her, he told himself, and I sent her away. That was a terrible thing to say to her. He remembered her tears, and how she had slowly sat down again on the bench.

And I came back to the hotel, he said aloud. And here I am sitting alone, thinking of her.

He got up and went into the kitchen. It was the middle of the afternoon and no one was there. Everyone was asleep. There was a small room beyond, in the garden, where he sometimes went, and where he kept most of his clothes. He opened the door and went in. There were two liters of wine on the table. He shut the door and sat down. He wanted to drink and pretend that the world did not exist.

Instead, he drank and thought about his wife, and he began to sob as he remembered that he had had a wife and a child, and that he had left her and she had taken the child away. And he saw her married again, with the father not loving the boy, and the boy unhappy. He might not even be sent to school, so that when he grew up he would never have any work, and then he would become a criminal. Mina won't care what happens to him, he thought. Her heart is dead.

He had finished the two bottles of wine. Now he got up and went to the kitchen to get two more. He came back through the garden, sobbing, thinking that he did not know whether he was alive in the world, or only remembering being alive after he had died. He was not sure whether he was a man or a shadow. He went on swallowing wine, thinking and weeping. Until now he had never thought of what the boy's life might be like. He might be hungry and cold. His mother would not put any good ideas into his head or good feelings into his heart.

She's bound to ruin him, he thought. I can't let her! I've got to get him away from her! He emptied the third bottle, and began on the fourth. If only I'd thrown her out and taken him right after he was born.

There was a knock at the door of the little room. Mohammed opened it. Mr. David stood there.

What's the matter? he wanted to know. Why are you crying?

I am not, said Mohammed. I was thinking.

Thinking? What about?

Mohammed did not answer. Mr. David was quiet for a moment. Then he said: I've got to go in and open the bar. It's late.

Mohammed wandered out through the kitchen and

into the bar, very drunk. It was hot that night, and there were a great many people wanting drinks. They bought him more drinks, and this went on until almost daylight. The people went home, and Mr. David said he was going in to bed. But Mohammed stayed on by himself in the bar, still drinking.

Mr. David got up at noon, went out into the garden, and did some exercises. Then he walked into the bar. Mohammed was sitting at a table with a bottle of Marqués de Riscal. What's going on? he said. Haven't you slept yet?

No, said Mohammed.

Why not? And you're still drinking?

Yes.

But why?

I've got nothing left, Mohammed told him. It was hard for him to speak. I'm tired of being in the world. I feel as if I were going to die.

What do you expect? cried Mr. David. With that mixture of drinks and no sleep? Of course you feel awful.

Alcohol has no effect on me, said Mohammed.

Mr. David laughed.

I'm different from other people. When I feel, I feel from my heart. Other people just feel. When I love, I love from my heart.

And who do you love now? said Mr. David.

She's gone and I'll never find her. I've lost everything. I don't exist. I won't live much longer.

Mohammed, stop all this! said Mr. David. You'll go to other places, meet other people, have a whole different life. Everything will be new and you'll forget about it.

I'll never forget. How could anyone forget? When you've had a girl like the one I had? You didn't know Mina. I was crazy ever to let her go.

You had to, said Mr. David. And remember how you got her. For a few hairs. You were lucky. Lucky to get her and lucky to get rid of her. Come on. Get up, and go in to bed. I'm going to give you a pill that will make you sleep.

Ouakha.

Mr. David went into the bathroom and brought out a red capsule. Mohammed took it with a swallow of water, and went into Mr. David's bedroom. Mr. David helped him undress, and Mohammed got into bed. The light that came through the blinds was very dim. Mr. David stood looking down at him for a moment, and went out. He shut the door softly.

59

MOHAMMED SLEPT FOR twenty-four hours. When he got up the next afternoon he opened the door and stepped out into the garden. The sun seemed very bright. He heard voices in the bar and went to the door. Mr. David was sitting with some Americans. When he saw Mohammed in his pyjamas with his hair rumpled and his eyes almost shut, he stood up.

Mohammed!

What's happened? cried Mohammed.

Nothing.

Something's happened. Hasn't somebody come to ask for me?

No, nobody. And Mr. David began to look worried.

Mohammed went out into the garden, and Mr. David turned to his friends. That boy's losing his mind, he said. There's something wrong with him. He's been very strange lately.

Mohammed went back into the bedroom and sat down on the edge of the bed. He held his head between his hands and looked down at the fur rug under his feet. What's happened? he thought. What have I been doing? What was I saying just now? Where have I been? Who have I been with? Who was it?

Mr. David came into the bedroom. How do you feel, Mohammed? What's the matter?

Where have I been? said Mohammed, looking up at him. Who have I been with? Who was I just talking to?

You were talking to me, said Mr. David. You haven't been anywhere. And he told him everything he had done the day before. That's right, said Mohammed. I remember. He stood up and put on his clothes. Then he had a glass of coffee and went out into the street. He wanted to go to his father's house in Mstakhoche. It was a long time since he had been to see his family. He walked up to the Zoco de Fuera and waited for the bus.

His little brother opened the door when he knocked. He kissed all his brothers and sisters. And his father's wife came in and greeted him. He sat with them, and they said: Why don't you come and see us any more? Where have you been?

At the hotel. There are a lot of tourists. There's been no time at all.

It's not right, what you do to your father, said his father's wife. Staying away so long.

I know, said Mohammed. But remember what he did to me.

He was right! she told him. That girl's worthless. She's no good for you. Are you still with her?

Mohammed looked down. I haven't seen her in a long time. A long, long time.

Your father's going to be very glad to hear that.

Then Mohammed called to each of his brothers and sisters, and gave each one a little money. And he handed some to his father's wife, and went out.

Almost as soon as he had shut the door he met Mina's father.

Well, Mohammed! How are you? How have you been?

As they talked, Si Ahmed suddenly said: It would have been better if you'd taken the baby. We ought to have helped you. If we'd talked with Mina she might have let you have him. But her mother wouldn't do it. Now she's gone off somewhere with a soldier. We don't know where she is.

Mohammed did not answer for a moment. Then he said: And she took the baby.

Yes, son, said Si Ahmed. It's too bad. I'm glad to see you looking so well.

She wanted to go, said Mohammed.

They said good-bye, and he went on his way down the street, leaving Si Ahmed standing at the door of his house.

60

ONE DAY MOHAMMED and Mr. David were sitting alone in the bar drinking whisky together. Mr. David drank more these days. He thought it was a way of keeping Mohammed in the hotel with him.

I've got to get out of this town, Mohammed was saying. I can't stay here any longer. Every time I go out I see something that reminds me of Mina. It's driving me crazy.

Did you ever go back and pay the witch in Beni Makada, when she got rid of Mina for you? Mr. David asked him.

I'm not rid of her! cried Mohammed. She's all I can think of. It didn't work. I want to think of something else.

There's nothing you can do about it, then, said Mr. David.

I can go to some other country and work. I could have a whole different life.

You can do that without leaving Tangier, Mr. David told him.

How?

You Moslems have holy men, don't you? They can change your ideas for you. There are all kinds of things they can do to keep you from thinking of her.

Mohammed was not listening. It was her mother who did it, he said. She got hold of something very strong.

You can stay here perfectly well, Mr. David went on. You're here in the hotel with me. You just stay on, and when I sell it we'll go to England. I can take you along with me. You can live there with me and work if you like, and you'll forget about all this.

He saw that Mohammed was paying no attention. He was muttering to himself as he poured another glass of whisky.

You could be having a good time, Mr. David told him. But you'd rather lie around and feel sorry for yourself. What happened between you and Mina is finished. It's all over. But you're still young! Eighteen isn't old.

I'm nineteen, said Mohammed. He tried to fill Mr. David's glass. Mr. David put his hand over it and shook his head.

You're not, he said. Not yet. You haven't seen the world. And you're wasting your life sitting here thinking about something that's been finished a long time. You say you have no friends, and nobody wants to see you. Look at you! Who wants to see anybody that looks the way you do, with your face half white and half black, and your hair that hasn't been cut for months, and those clothes!

Mohammed said nothing. He drank his whisky slowly and looked at the other side of the room. Mr. David poured himself a little whisky. He was thinking that perhaps he had said too much. He spoke now more gently.

You're such a fine, good boy. Everyone loves you. When people come into the bar, if you're not there, they always want to know where you are. At least, they did until you got this way, until you forgot how to joke and laugh and be happy. But who wants to look at somebody who's dirty and drunk and angry? You come into the hotel without speaking to anybody and go into that little room. Then you come out drunk and wander out again into the street. You stay all night in some bar or café. You get no sleep. You feel sick. If you go on like this another year or two, you're going to end either in the hospital or the cemetery. Look at Englishmen! When they love a girl and something happens and they lose her, they go right on with their lives. They forget about her. Later they may even meet her in the street and not know who she is. They find one better than the one they lost.

Englishmen are cold, said Mohammed. They don't feel anything.

You could get up, went on Mr. David, and go in and take a bath and shave, and go and get your hair cut, and put on some clean clothes. And then you could go out and find a better girl than you've ever had in your life. And she could give you something new. Then if you should see Mina you wouldn't even look at her.

Mohammed started to pour himself more whisky. Mr. David frowned at him and he stopped.

You've got a hard head, Mohammed. Most Moroccans have. They say: I'll do it, but they don't do it. You tell them: Do this. And they do something different. A man's got to use his head. He's got to listen to words and try to understand them. He's got to be able to look at the other person and know what he's telling him, and say: Yes, that's true. And if he doesn't agree, he's got to say: No. That's not true. Am I right or wrong?

You're right, said Mohammed. But what do I do?

You look into the mirror.

Mohammed got up and walked slowly into the bathroom. He ran the hot water and took a long bath. Then he shaved and dressed in a clean shirt and a pair of well-pressed trousers, and went out to the barber's shop.

He was pleased with the way he looked when he came back to the hotel. Mr. David sat with an American in the bar. Look at that! he cried as Mohammed came in. He followed Mohammed with his eyes as he walked around the room watching himself in the mirror.

It makes me feel so good to see you looking like this again, said Mr. David. Now it's a pleasure to look

194

at you. He turned to the American and said: Do you see Mohammed? He's a boy again. More handsome than ever.

Thank you, said Mohammed. He was tidying up the bar. His body felt very light, and he was happy everywhere in it. And he laughed and drank all evening with the Nazarenes who came in.

Late at night he shut the bar. Mr. David was waiting for him in the garden. How do you feel now? he asked Mohammed as he came out.

Better.

What did I tell you?

Yes. You were right. I've thought about what you said. I feel better. Not well yet, but better.

In a few days you'll be fine.

Yes.

Mr. David put a pile of records on the phonograph and they went to bed.

61

MOHAMMED WENT ON living with Mr. David at the hotel and helping him in the bar, and they were both happy. In different ways Mr. David often told him that everything he had predicted for him had come true. The memory of Mina had gone out of his head. Because he was happy he drank less and grew healthy again. He had other girls, but he did not let himself love any of them. When he thought about it he would say to himself: I'm lucky to have a friend who understands the world. He pulled me back when I was at the edge.

The years went by.

One rainy morning Mohammed stood in the bus shelter in the Zoco de Fuera waiting for a bus to Mstakhoche. He had bought some fruit to take to his family. As he stood there, he noticed a country woman in a dirty haik staring at him. She had two small children with her, and a baby strapped on her back. He looked at her for a long moment, but she did not lower her eyes. It was he who looked away first.

An instant later he turned back. She was still looking at him. The bus drove up and the people pushed in. The woman got in ahead of him with the children clinging to her haik.

Everything in the bus was wet. The woman sat down, and Mohammed sat opposite her, because the seat was still vacant. People were running through the aisle to find places to sit. As the bus climbed the hill by the French Consulate, he glanced again at the woman, and saw that she was crying behind her veil.

Maybe I look like someone in her family, he thought. Someone who's dead, perhaps.

She leaned towards him and spoke in a low voice.

Don't you know me, Mohammed?

No.

Then he said: Are you Mina?

Yes.

Allah! Is it really you? I can't believe it. Her face was bony and the skin on it was yellow.

Then he turned around to the seat behind him where she had put the two children. Are they yours?

Yes.

The big one is Driss?

She nodded.

Mohammed turned around further. Do you go to school, Driss? he asked the little boy.

I go to the mcid.

Good! And they teach you the Koran. I like boys who know the Koran.

When the bus arrived at the end of the line they got out. Let's go over there under the trees and talk a minute, said Mohammed.

They walked under the eucalyptus trees and sat down. The ground was wet.

Mina, what's happened? I don't understand how you can look like this.

She burst into tears, and Mohammed did not want to see it. He got to his feet. Mina and the children followed him back to the street.

Mohammed stooped down and put his arms around the small boy. He took out a five thousand franc note and handed it to him.

Go and get something nice, he told him. Good-bye, Mina.

He kissed the child and went on quickly to his father's house.